A
COVINGTON
CHRISTMAS

A COVINGTON CHRISTMAS

JOAN MEDLICOTT

POCKET BOOKS

New York   London   Toronto   Sydney

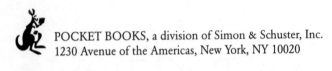

POCKET BOOKS, a division of Simon & Schuster, Inc.
1230 Avenue of the Americas, New York, NY 10020

Library of Congress Cataloging-in-Publication Data is available.

ISBN-13: 978-0-7434-9921-7
ISBN-10:   0-7434-9921-2

First Pocket Books trade paperback edition November 2005

10 9 8 7 6 5 4 3 2 1

POCKET and colophon are registered trademarks of
Simon & Schuster, Inc.

Manufactured in the United States of America

For information regarding special discounts for bulk purchases,
please contact Simon & Schuster Special Sales at 1-800-456-6798
or business@simonandschuster.com.

*To Louis Miles in gratitude for his
generous contribution of time and information
pertaining to Cove Road Church and the weddings,
and to Celia Miles for her support,
critical eye, and friendship.*

Acknowledgment

Thanks to Dianne La Forge for the idea.

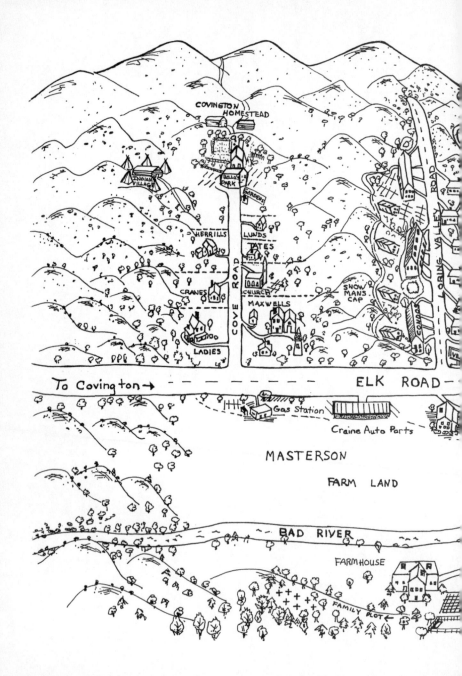

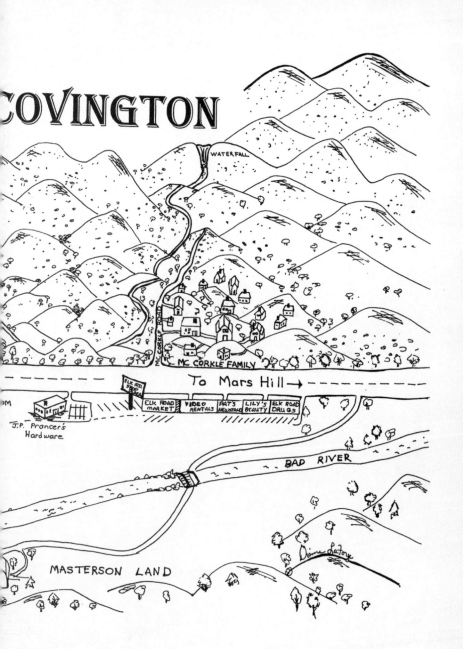

A
COVINGTON
CHRISTMAS

1

֍

The October day was bright, invigorating, and cool enough for a light jacket. Wine-colored dogwood leaves heralded the muted colors of a North Carolina fall: peach, plum, rust, cinnamon, and an array of yellows.

Grace Singleton stepped from the porch of the farmhouse she shared with her friends, Amelia Declose and Hannah Parrish. Walking briskly, she traversed the lawn, crossed Cove Road, and turned left down the road to the church, where she had agreed to help young Pastor Denny Ledbetter clean out the church's attic.

As she climbed the narrow pull-down stairs leading from the storage room off the pastor's office, Grace heard Denny Ledbetter's alarmed voice.

"Good heavens. This is impossible! It's just terrible!"

"What's impossible?" she asked, sticking her head into the dim attic.

Pervaded by a musty odor, the attic was a dank, dusty

room without ventilation other than the slatted ovals em-
bedded in opposite walls. Two bare bulbs crusted with dust
dangled on ancient wires from the ceiling. Denny sat cross-
legged in the middle of the room, fenced by boxes.

"This." He held out a folder and waved it in her direction. Fine dust wafted toward her and Grace sneezed.
Denny did as well, five, six, seven times, one quick jerk of a
sneeze after the other.

He pointed to the boxes around him. "Most of this stuff
is disposable, mainly bank statements dating from the late
1970s and 1980s. But then I found this. It's shocking and
unbelievable. Come, read it. You won't believe it. It's very
upsetting." He pulled several deeply creased letters from the
folder and handed them to her. "Mrs. Singleton, if what this
letter says is true, it's explosive."

"Call me Grace, please. Everyone does."

Grateful that she had remembered to slip them into the
pocket of her jacket, Grace pulled out her reading glasses.
Dated December 1, 1963, the letter was written on fine
parchment yellowed with age, and addressed to Griffen
Anson, Chairman of the Cove Road Community Church
Council, Covington, North Carolina. The content was startling, and brief, and Grace read aloud.

Dear Mr. Anson,
We regret to inform you that Richard W. Simms has
not been granted a degree from the seminary, and
therefore the presbytery, which recommended Mr.
Simms for seminary training, will not allow his ordi-

nation. Mr. Simms is thus not authorized to perform baptisms, weddings, or other rites and ceremonies, or to conduct services or to be deemed a pastor. Many fine young men have been graduated, and we would be pleased to assist you in your search for a pastor for your congregation.

Sincerely yours,
John P. Garner, President
McLeod Theological Seminary in Ohio

Attached with a rusted staple was a copy of another letter from the presbytery executive, confirming the fact that without a seminary degree Simms could not be ordained. Neither letter contained an explanation as to why Simms had failed to graduate.

"What is a presbytery executive?" Grace asked.

"Simms must have been a Presbyterian, and this letter is from the churchman who was overseeing his training and ordination. Something quite serious must have happened for them to dismiss him and not ordain him."

Grace handed Denny the letters and removed her glasses. "These letters are over forty years old. How could this be?" Did Pastor Johnson know about this? No, he couldn't possibly have known. These events took place before his tenure as pastor. And if he had known, surely he wouldn't have kept such information secret all the years he'd been here.

Denny shuffled several documents. "There's more. These are unsigned marriage certificates for the Craines, the

Herrills, and three couples named McCorkle. Simms married them all between October and November of 1963. The church called him to service and installed him before they got these letters, I guess, and dear Lord, Simms never filed these marriages with the court." His eyes widened. "You know what this means, Grace?"

"I'm not sure."

Denny smoothed the yellowed papers on the top of a box. "The couples Simms married were never really married, and he knew that. And whoever this Anson was, he knew it, too, and apparently chose to say nothing about it." Denny stared at the far wall as he tapped the letters with his fingers. "I'm sure Pastor Johnson has never seen these. He told me that he'd never bothered with anything in the attic."

Aghast, Grace stared at him. "This means that Frank and Alma Craine, Velma and Charlie Herrill, are not married?"

"They must have gotten licenses and blood tests. But these certificates are supposed to represent legal proof of their marriages by a bona fide minister, and they were never recorded. The couples whom Simms married were not then, and are not now, married in the eyes of a church, or even legally at the courthouse." His hands fell heavily on top of the letters. "I'm just dumbfounded that Anson knew about this and didn't tell anyone. He must have shown them to Simms, must have suggested or insisted that he leave. Then apparently he shoved all this information in a box and stuck it up here. Why would he do that?"

"What will you do?" Grace asked. "These couples have

lived all these years thinking that they're married. Will you throw the certificates and the letters away, or will you tell them about this? And Pastor Johnson?"

"He's not well; I don't want to upset him. And I can't begin to imagine the trouble this would cause if it became public knowledge. I need to think about this. I'll pray on it for a few days."

"Surely they're considered married under common law," Grace said hopefully. "Many states recognize such marriages. What would be the point of telling these five couples now, after all these years?"

Denny sneezed again and again; his eyes reddened and grew teary. "I'm not sure North Carolina is a common-law state. I'll have to check that out. We'd better call it a day; my dust allergy is getting worse by the minute. I've been up here too long."

They descended the unsteady stairs, and Denny shoved the stairwell up into the ceiling with a thud. He had met Grace only once in passing, and had liked her clear brown eyes. Honest, he'd thought. He had also noted the faint scent of vanilla and cinnamon that floated about her. She was a terrific cook, Pastor Johnson had told him. Denny judged her to be the age of a grandmother, though her hair was brown, not gray, and her round face was remarkably un-lined. He was glad that she was the one Pastor Johnson had suggested that he ask to help him clear out the attic.

As they walked to the front of the church, Grace asked, "How ill is Pastor Johnson? Be honest with me, please. He isn't dying, is he? It's not some drawn-out terminal illness?"

Denny shook his head. "We know it's not cancer or heart failure, and it's not his kidneys. His doctor seems to think he's just worn out. He's eighty-seven years old. We worry he'll fall. He's slowed down considerably, as you know."

"Yes, I can see that. He uses a cane now."

"At times his memory fails him. I've seen him go blank, smack in the middle of a service, over words he's spoken hundreds of times." Pastor Denny's voice dropped. "Recently he forgot the name of a baby he was christening, right after the father whispered the child's name in his ear."

"I worry about my own memory," she replied.

"So do I." He laughed. "I make it a point to repeat names. It's so important that a pastor remember everyone's name."

Grace looked up at Denny, who at five feet eight inches was considerably taller than she was. "We're all glad that you're here for Pastor Johnson."

"Thank you. I'm humbled at having been asked to join him and assist him with his duties. I hope I'll be worthy."

"I'm sure you are. Even though you've only been here a few weeks, folks say such nice things about you. They especially enjoy your sermons."

Charlie Herrill, head of the Cove Road Church Council, had told Grace that Denny was thirty-one years old and had already served his first congregation for six years. At Pastor Johnson's request, Charlie had gone down to South Carolina, where Denny was pastor, and asked the young man to come and work with Pastor Johnson.

"Pastor Johnson came into my life when I was seven

years old and in the orphanage," Denny said. "Each summer, he served as chaplain at a summer camp the orphanage ran. He singled me out, became, in effect, my surrogate father. He encouraged me through high school, and sent me to college and seminary. I could never refuse him anything—not even if Lorna had agreed to marry me." He stopped and looked away, shrugged, then met Grace's eyes. "Lorna said she couldn't imagine herself as a pastor's wife, and frankly that told me she didn't feel about me the way I felt about her."

"I'm sorry," Grace said.

"It's all right. So many marriages end in divorce, and I avoided that. If it's the Lord's plan for me, the right person will come along one of these days."

Emboldened by his honesty and the sadness in his blue eyes, Grace stretched up and kissed his cheek. "I wish you the very best. You're a good man, Denny Ledbetter. I'll leave you to pray on your decision about those letters."

Out on Cove Road, Grace breathed deeply and filled her lungs with crisp fall air. She felt slightly dizzy, and wondered whether it was due to all that dust, the distressing information they had uncovered, or the uncertainty as to what Pastor Ledbetter would do about the letters. For a moment she stood there, then turned right toward Bella's Park, two blocks farther down the road, where she was certain she would find Hannah.

Denny stood in the center of Cove Road, hands on hips, and stared up at the church. Though small, it was well proportioned, with a steeple that was neither too short nor too tall. The church really needed a face-lift. The smoke from the fire that had burned the homes of Grace and her house-mates, the Craines, and the Herrills two years ago had turned the white clapboard a murky gray. He couldn't do the job himself, since he'd fallen off a ladder while painting his former church hall. Six weeks in a cast had been fol-lowed by as many weeks of arduous physical therapy, and his leg still ached with every change of weather. The experi-ence had taught him about pain and patience. Life is most capricious, Denny thought. Yet he trusted that God knew best.

Walking slowly back to the cottage behind the church, where he lived with Pastor Johnson, Denny recalled the day that Charlie Herrill had arrived in South Carolina. It was the day after Lorna had rejected him and broken his heart.

"I'm a bit uncomfortable with this," Charlie had said. "I'm fully aware that you're not seeking a new church or wanting to make a change, but you're very special to Pastor Johnson. He speaks of you as if you were his son. When was the last time you saw him?"

"Last summer."

"You'd be shocked at how frail he's become. We worry about him living alone."

Guilt had swept over Denny. How long had it been since they had talked or written? Months, he realized. He'd been so wrapped up in Lorna and work that he had ne-glected his former mentor. "Tell me, how sick is he?"

Charlie had settled his large frame into the chair in the

restaurant where they had gone for dinner, flipped open his napkin, and spread it across his lap. "Well, if you'd seen him strumming a banjo at our neighborhood party this past summer, you'd have thought he'd go on forever. But I'm afraid that's not the case. After that spurt of energy, he's been ailing with one thing and another ever since." Charlie shook his head. "We're real concerned about him. He's been with our church so long, he's like family to us."

"He's like family to me," Denny replied.

"We don't want to ask him to retire. For years he's been solid and reliable to the core. He's dedicated his life to our small congregation, given us too many good years of service for us to put him out to pasture. We'd rather wait until he suggests retirement—but right now, with Christmas coming, he needs help, and we need a minister." Charlie had cleared his throat. "Pastor Ledbetter, we'd like you to come look after him, work with him, learn our ways, and when he leaves for whatever reason, if you like us and we like you, you can step right in."

The waiter had appeared and they'd ordered their dinners.

"Covington's a small town," Charlie continued. "Asheville's the closest city, about thirty-five minutes' drive. But we're the kind of place where you can settle in, raise a family, and feel you're a part of the community."

Denny weighed both sides of the situation. This church had hired him right out of the seminary, had taken a chance on him, given him space and time to grow into his robes. He had cut his pastoral teeth, so to speak, with these fine folks. But larger issues of loyalty and unconditional love, freely given to a young boy who had so desperately needed that love and affection, and concerns about gratitude, trust, and repayment of a debt, left no doubt in Denny's mind that he would say yes to Charlie Herrill.

Charlie was now talking money. "I realize we probably can't pay you near what you're making now, and you'd have to live in the parsonage with Pastor Johnson. It's small, but it has two bedrooms."

Denny knew the parsonage from his visits. It was small, but Pastor Johnson was neat and considerate of others, and Denny had no concerns about sharing a home with him. "Money is the least of it. I'd be honored to help take care of him and help in any way I can."

When he handed in his resignation, the church council and many members of his congregation had protested. The council offered him an increase in salary and a vehicle. Denny explained how Pastor Johnson had been there for him all of his life, and that there was no choice. Love, gratitude, and obligation called him to Covington.

They said they understood, but when they shook his hand in farewell, some shook their heads as if he were a son who had disappointed them. Many of the women cried. Some hugged him so tightly, he thought they'd squeeze the breath out of him.

The hardest had been Lorna's mother, who had taken him aside and said, "I regret my daughter's decision. She's a fool. We would have liked to have you for our son-in-law." She'd hugged him. "You be well, now, and find you a nice

girl who'll be right for you." It had taken all his strength
that day not to cling to her and cry.

Denny now walked past the cottage to the small cemetery of gray tombstones. Graveyards had always attracted
him, and he visited them wherever he went. Sometimes on
warm summer days, Pastor Johnson walked with him there.
But the ground was uneven, and even with his cane, the
old pastor found it hard to negotiate the paths. "Ah,
Denny, my boy," he'd said recently, "you live long enough,
you regress until you're right back to where you were as an
infant."

Talk of that nature depressed Denny; the thought of losing the pastor filled him with dread and a great sadness.

Grace had said, when he'd first met her, that her son's
former partner, Charles Cawley, was buried in their cemetery. He searched for the stone, which she described as
slightly canted. She intended to have it straightened, she
had said.

"Last winter, with all the thawing and freezing, the
ground heaved and tilted the stone," she had explained. "I
feel bad for not having taken care of it during the summer. I
kept waiting for my son, Roger, to come up from South
Carolina. I visited him there several times, but he didn't
come up here. Seems to me they could make the stones
longer and bury them deeper so they'd be impervious to
weather changes, wouldn't you think?"

She had also told him that she liked tombstones that
said something about the deceased and didn't just list a
name and dates.

"I've written down what I want on my stone when the time comes," she had said.

"And what is that, if I may ask?"

" 'She listened well and was a trustworthy friend.' "

"How very fine that is," Denny had replied, and she had smiled.

He'd never given such matters much thought, but found he agreed with her as he stood over the tilted stone, which read:

> **Charles Louis Cawley, born Isle of Wight, England**
> **Died in America, a long way from home.**
> **Honest. Loving. Beloved. He is missed.**

As usual, Pastor Johnson had been right: Denny liked Grace Singleton very much, indeed.

2

The sign over Hannah's office read DIRECTOR OF GAR-
DENS, a position she'd never dreamed she would hold in her
mid-seventies. But Hannah, with her angular build and fea-
tures, had more vitality and creativity than many a younger
person. The exhibition gardens she had developed in the
last few years were increasingly visited by tourists to the
area, local people, and schoolchildren. Classes were offered
in gardening for both adults and children. Brenda Tate, the
principal of Caster Elementary School, had prevailed on
Hannah to teach a gardening class at school, and this had
led to a children's garden at Bella's Park, which they planted
and maintained all summer long.

Hannah's mind seemed never to stop; she was always
planning. "My workmen and I are going to tackle a trail up
into the woods and plant a woodland garden next spring,
and maybe a moss garden. Moss gardens are quite beautiful," she had recently told Grace and Amelia. "You can't

walk on them or you'll kill the moss, but they feel so good to the hand and are peaceful to look at."

Grace knocked on Hannah's door. She'd seen Amelia, Hannah's foreman, Tom, Charlie Herrill, Max, and others barge into Hannah's office without knocking, but she considered that rude and disrespectful, though Hannah had never complained about it.

"Come in," Hannah called.

When Grace entered, Hannah asked, "What's the matter, Grace? Your eyes are all red."

"A reaction to the dust in that church attic."

"But your brow's furrowed, and your mouth's all puckered. That from dust, too?" Hannah smiled.

Grace dropped onto the sofa across the room, and Hannah set aside her work, left her desk, and joined Grace.

"What's the problem? Something with Bob or Amelia?"

"I only wish. That would be easy." Grace nibbled the edge of her lower lip. She had to tell somebody or burst. "This is confidential. Promise me you won't tell anyone— not even Max."

Hannah rested her right hand over her heart. "I won't, I promise. Not even Max."

Without hesitation, then, Grace plunged into her story about helping Pastor Ledbetter clean out the attic and finding the letters concerning Simms.

"That's quite something," Hannah said. "Griffen Anson wanted that information and his part in it buried. I'm surprised that he didn't just tear up those letters and be done with it. I hope the new minister's not so self-righteous that he feels he's got to tell these couples the truth, and get everyone in Covington in a tizzy. Can you imagine that old gossip, Alma Craine, being able to handle other people gossiping about her for a change?"

"No, I can't. I can't even begin to imagine how Velma and Charlie and the others would react, or what they would do about it."

"I say he ought to let sleeping dogs lie," Hannah said. "After all these years, even if they were never legally married, they'd be common-law husbands and wives."

"Denny isn't sure North Carolina's a common-law state. Not all states consider long-term live-in relationships legal. I'm not sure how that applies or doesn't in a situation like this. These folks have been, or thought they were, married for forty years," Grace said. "They'd have to consult a lawyer, which would be very upsetting as well as expensive. Remember, these folks have a different ethic than you and I do about such things. They'd want to be legally married."

Hannah's smile curled the edges of her mouth. "We do have peculiar relationships with Max and Bob, don't we? Try as he will, Bob can't get you to marry him or even to live with him. Max proposed marriage for financial reasons, so he could leave me his property and I won't have to pay taxes on it when he dies, assuming he dies before I do—and he said I can still live at home and we can go on just as we are now." She sighed. "Though I told him I'd marry him at the end of this month, I've been rethinking it. I told Max yesterday that I'm just not ready."

"I cannot believe you've changed that date, Hannah. How could you, after taking so long to set one?"

Hannah shrugged. "It wasn't hard to do, considering that when we do get married, it's going to be fast and easy, probably at the courthouse. No fuss, no bother."

"How'd Max take it? He's been so anxious to get married."

"He was a bit perturbed at first, but said he'll wait until spring. Afterward, I have every intention of living at home with you and Amelia. So my relationship with Max is an even stranger arrangement than yours is with Bob."

"Well, our neighbors have come to accept us as peculiar Yankees," Grace replied. "But I do believe they'd be very upset if they discovered *they've* been living together unmarried in the eyes of God and their church all these years." She frowned. "And in the eyes of the law."

"That's probably true," Hannah said. "We'll just have to wait and see what happens."

That evening Max and Hannah, Grace and Bob, drove to Asheville to a new seafood restaurant. Several years ago when they had first met, the two men had little in common and little reason to become friends. Bob Richardson was retired from the army, stiff at times, sometimes autocratic, but quite sweet underneath. Tall, husky George Maxwell, called Max, operated a dairy farm across the road from the ladies' house, and he owned and operated Bella's Park. Over time the men had adjusted to their differences and become friends; they watched the Super Bowl together, and enjoyed evenings out as a foursome.

Years after Max's wife, Bella, had died, their son, Zachary, had rejected his father's business and whatever inheritance there would be, married an Indian woman without sending an invitation to the wedding to Max, and moved to India to join his father-in-law's import-export business.

Max and Hannah's relationship had developed slowly as they worked together. It was after Zachary's blunt and rude dismissal of his father and all he stood for that Max had decided to leave his estate to Hannah, and to assure the tax benefits to her, he asked her to marry him. It had taken Hannah almost a year to give Max a yes to his proposal. Although the ladies spent great quantities of time with these men, they remained true to their original commitment to share a home with each other and with Amelia.

Once settled in at the cozy, upscale restaurant, they ordered wine. Because of her diabetes, Grace ordered unsweetened iced tea. Then Bob asked, "So, Grace, did you and the new minister get the attic cleaned out?"

"Heavens, no. It's far from finished. There were dozens of dusty boxes filled with old bank statements. We sneezed our heads off."

"No skeletons in the church's closet?" Bob's casual question would have passed unnoticed, but for Grace's eyes seeking Hannah's. It was a giveaway, and Bob picked up on it. "What is it? What did you find? Did they cover up a murder?" He rubbed his hands together and leaned across the table.

Grace waved her hand as if to brush the thought aside. "Goodness, no. Nothing like that."

"But it's something, isn't it? What could it be? Max and I will guess, try to figure it out."

They delighted in naming one situation after the other: an illegitimate child, someone jailed for embezzlement of church funds, the church had hired and fired a gay minister.

Grace laughed and Hannah rolled her eyes at each scenario, and Grace shook her head. Their dinners arrived and they chatted about other things as they ate, but the guessing game began again while the men waited for their apple pie à la mode.

"Your cholesterol, Bob. Maybe you should let dessert go?" Grace suggested.

"You only live once," he replied. "You can't deprive yourself of everything. Once in a while, a treat won't hurt."

Or would it? So much went on inside of our bodies we had no clue about, Grace thought. How would she have known, for example, that her pancreas would stop working properly? The more Grace learned about the potential ill effects of diabetes on one's eyes (one could go blind), on one's extremities (one could lose a leg), and on one's heart and kidneys (they could fail), the more careful about sugar and carbohydrates, especially desserts, she had become. Increasingly, it was easier for her to say no to desserts. One slice of chocolate cake would shoot her sugar sky high and leave her mind fuzzy. She hated that feeling. Grace carried nuts—walnuts, cashews, and almonds were her favorites—in her purse and a handful between meals kept her blood sugar stable.

Bob returned to the "what's in the attic" game. "Something so sinister or so shameful that someone hid it away among a bunch of old papers in the attic. Now, what could that be?"

"You didn't find any bones up there, did you?" Max interjected with a twinkle in his eye.

"You haven't even come close," Grace replied.

"So, it's a big deal?" Max's eyes flashed. He, too, was obviously enjoying the game.

Grace nodded, caught up by their interest. "A very big deal."

"Does it affect one person, or two, or everyone who belongs to the church?" Max asked.

"What is this, twenty questions?" Hannah poked Grace's shoulder, and Grace sobered immediately. She'd hinted at too much.

"That's enough, game's over. It was just that, a game," Grace said. "You seemed to enjoy it, so I led you on."

"I don't believe that for a minute." Bob grinned mischievously. "Max and I will figure it out."

"I almost forgot," Grace said. "One thing I did find out is that Pastor Denny was jilted by a girl just before he came up here. The poor man proposed and was rejected. He's not over it, that's for sure. I can see the unhappiness in his eyes. We have to help him."

"Help him how?" Max asked.

"We'll introduce him to suitable young women." She turned to Bob and placed her hand over his. "Bob, there must be nice young women, seniors maybe, at the college."

Bob, who taught an evening class in American history at Mars Hill College, started to shake his head.

"Now, Bob, really. Can't you think of someone we might introduce the pastor to?"

"Oh, no you don't." He threw up his hands. "I'm not getting involved in anyone's love life. I've got enough trouble with my own."

"Oh, nonsense," Grace replied. "Your love life's never been better."

Bob grinned at her. "True. But I don't want to get in the middle of anyone else's business."

"What harm can it do just to introduce two people? Either they take to each other or they don't. That's not matchmaking; it's just a nice way to bring two people together."

"Have you ever heard of the Eleventh Commandment?" Bob asked.

"What Eleventh Commandment?"

"Thou shalt MYOB. Mind your own business."

Grace swatted his arm. "Bob, I always mind my own business. This is different."

The check arrived. Bob and Max divvied it up, paid, and soon they were on their way. The whole way back to Covington, Grace talked about who to introduce Denny to, and where and when so it wouldn't seem contrived.

3

The next day, while Pastor Denny deliberated about the letters, work in the attic continued.

Settling into a chair, Grace tugged at the taped folds of a box top, but it was strapped repeatedly with wide gray tape and would not be pulled apart by hand.

"Let me cut that for you." Denny stepped forward with a box cutter and sliced through the tape, freeing the folded tops, which snapped back, flipping dust into Grace's face. "Lord, I am sorry," he said.

"We ought to be handling this stuff with gloves," Grace said. Already her hands were discolored with a light layer of grime.

"You're right. I should have thought of that. Here, let me get those flaps out of your way." Denny sliced away the flaps.

"That's much better." Grace bent to the task. She removed long envelopes containing brittle bank statements and checks dating back to the 1970s and into the early 1980s. Many of the envelopes had been chewed around the edges by an intrepid insect.

"Some of these bank statements go back thirty years. The others are more like twenty years old." She held up an envelope.

"Out they go, then. Anything older than ten years, we'll dump. Here, I'll just shove that box closer to the steps and carry it down later."

With determination, Grace attacked the next box and thumbed through envelope after envelope, lifting every third one and squinting to read faded postmarks. "Nineteen seventy-seven. Nineteen seventy-nine."

Like bare feet on damp sand, the pastor's shoes left impressions in the dusty floor wherever he walked. Soon boxes accumulated at the top of the stairs. He carried several down, and when he returned, he sneezed as often as Grace did.

"I don't want you to get sick," he said. "Just say the word and we'll quit."

Grace was not ready to quit just yet. Scattered helter-skelter among the envelopes in the 1978 box were snapshots of people she did not recognize: four smiling women standing behind a long table brimming with cakes and pies, a county fair perhaps, and several pictures of a choir in long robes. When had this church had a choir? She'd never heard singing from the church, only carolers on Cove Road at Christmastime, and they came from the Methodist church farther down on Elk Road. Any choir Cove Road Church had had must have been disbanded long ago. In another faded photo, a group of men in suits and hats posed self-importantly on the church steps—church elders from another era?

Denny showed little interest in the pictures. "If no one's cared enough to keep them in an album, obviously they're not important," he said.

But Grace wondered if they might be of value to some-one—the church historian, perhaps, if there was one. "Don't throw them out just yet. Would you mind showing them to Pastor Johnson and see if he recognizes anyone? If not, I'll see if Velma Herrill does. Maybe there's a church album they could be added to."

She handed Denny the pictures, which he slipped into his shirt pocket. Then he lugged that box to join the grow-ing pile at the top of the stairs. Soon he made a second trip down and up.

As they worked, Denny's mind drifted, as it often did, to Lorna Atwell: round faced and dark eyed, a vision of all he considered beautiful in a woman. She was also the pam-pered daughter of one of the members of his former church council.

Denny's experience with girls had been limited to a heartbreaking crush at the orphanage when he was fourteen, and later to a fellow student he had dated casually during his last year at college. And then, Lorna graduated from Elon College over near Greensboro, North Carolina, and came home. She breezed into his life at a church picnic, all smiles and laughter, and captured his heart, which in time he would discover she held far too lightly.

For six months, Denny had escorted Lorna to every social event at the country club where her folks belonged, to
picnics and dances at the church, to a Christian convention
in Columbia. They attended movies and shared popcorn.
They held hands as they roamed the exhibits at the state
fair. They sat jammed close on bleachers and cheered intrepid riders at the rodeo. Denny had considered them to be a
couple. Obviously she had not.

But why was he tormenting himself like this? Enough
time had been wasted on Lorna.

He turned to Grace and set another box before her. His
leg was beginning to hurt from the dampness and the
climbing up and down the stairs. He sat down and wiped
his hands on his pants.

"How long have you lived in Covington?"

"Almost six years, but it seems as if I've been here forever. And I mean that in the best possible sense. We love it
here, Hannah, Amelia, and I. We've put down roots, and
we've changed, grown, built new lives in Covington.

"Brenda Tate and her husband, Harold, were the first
people we met, and they were so good to us. Harold was a
friend of Amelia's cousin, the one who left her the house.
He showed us all around the place and found us a good
builder for the repairs. He even kept an eye on the work
when we returned to Pennsylvania to close out our affairs
and pack up."

She stopped working and stared into space, remembering. "What a mess that old farmhouse was. The steps and
porch tilted, and the roof leaked. Many of the floorboards

inside were rotten. You should have seen that kitchen; it was the epitome of old-fashioned. There was one bathroom upstairs for all four bedrooms, and there was even a possum living in the walls, if you can believe that."

"A possum in the walls of your house? That must have been most unpleasant."

Grace slapped her palms on her knees and laughed. "It was, indeed. Quite a shock, and scary, too. Amelia heard it first, the knocking and scurrying. It scared us out of our wits until we knew what it was, and were assured that we could call people in Asheville who'd come out, set a trap for it, and take it away, which they did.

"I miss Harold. Unfortunately, he passed away about three years ago from lung cancer. He had refused for over a year to see a doctor, and when he finally went and they found the cancer, they discovered that it was advanced, a stage four cancer. Just a couple of months, and he was gone. It was a great loss for his wife, Brenda, and for all his friends."

"I'm so sorry. I've heard about him. People held him in high regard."

She nodded. "Yes, they did."

Denny changed the subject. "After you settled in, did you find people around here friendly?"

"It was mainly the Tates who befriended us at first. Other folks were polite but distant, like in any small town, I imagine. It takes time to get to know folks, and for them to get to know you and accept you. And then we had the fire. As terrible as it was, it brought us closer to everyone on Cove Road."

"It's a shame that it takes a tragedy to bring people together. When exactly was the fire?"

"Let's see. Two years ago in the summer, a long drought left the woods like tinder. Brad Herrill, Charlie and Velma's youngest boy, dropped a lit cigarette on the ground one night when he came home from a party, and the sheriff thought that started the whole thing."

"That must have been so distressing for the Herrills, that their son could have started a terrible fire."

"It was. Charlie insisted that Brad tell the sheriff about the cigarette, but the police didn't charge him. Everything was so dry. How could they be sure it was his cigarette that caused the fire?"

"And since then, the church has never been painted," Denny mused aloud. "The white exterior's gone gray from the smoke, and the interior still has the smell of smoke, although Pastor Johnson tells me the ladies gave the pews and floors a good scrubbing."

"Yes, they scrubbed and scrubbed. But smoke permeates everything and won't let go easily," Grace said. "The air around here smelled of smoke and ash long after the remains of the houses were razed." She shuddered, reliving that time. "Even when we started to rebuild, you could walk by and the odors from that fire were still there. Occasionally even now, I get a whiff of it. Hannah tells me it's my imagination, but I've always been sensitive to smells."

They fell silent, then, sorting through the boxes.

"If I may ask, in what ways have your lives changed since you came here?" Denny asked.

Grace paused a moment to consider this, and Denny sliced away the flaps of the box that sat before her. "Well, we've made wonderful new friends. We've all revived old interests. I always wanted to be a teacher, and now I tutor kids at Caster Elementary School. I'm good friends with a very nice man, the grandfather of a boy I tutored. That was the last thing I expected to happen after losing my husband. Maybe you've met him, Bob Richardson? Through him and Tyler's father, Russell, and his second wife, Emily, I have a whole new extended family. Tyler's mother was killed in a car crash. Bob's grandkids—Tyler, who's a teenager now, and Melissa, his two-and-a-half-year-old sister—are like my own."

"I don't think I've had the pleasure of meeting Mr. Richardson."

"You'll meet Bob soon, I'm sure."

"Are you planning to be married?"

Grace set her hands on her hips. "When you've been the kind of wife I was, catering to my husband, doing what Ted wanted, being what he wanted, and then nursing him until he passed away, you don't want to take on another marriage. Bob and I have a fine understanding. We care deeply for each other. He's retired from the military and sort of formal, and he assumed I'd want to get married. It took a while to convince him that I didn't want to marry, but that I did love him. He's okay with it now, and has his own place, and folks around here have come to accept us just as we are."

"I respect your situation, and look forward to meeting Bob." They worked in silence again before Denny asked,

"And your friend Amelia? How have things changed for her?"

"Amelia changed a lot, too. Her husband's career came before all else. He was an executive with the International Red Cross, and they traveled extensively. There were social pressures on her to entertain his colleagues and people whose favors he curried for the benefit of his work. All her married life, Amelia set aside any interests of her own. After we were settled in Covington, she signed up for photography classes with Mike, a photographer in Weaverville. He's a very fine teacher and has become a good friend. To her great surprise, Amelia discovered not just a liking but a passion for photography, and she is excellent at it."

"She is, indeed. I have the pleasure of owning her book. Charlie Herrill sent it to me as an added incentive, I imagine, to come here."

"Amelia's been very successful. She's working on another coffee-table book. Her prints are sold in a gallery in New York."

"The photographs of the countryside and mountains around here are beautiful. Over the years I've come up to visit Pastor Johnson occasionally, and it's a lovely area."

"You came here, and I never met you?"

"We usually didn't stay in Covington. He'd take a few days off, and we'd drive over to Tennessee or up into West Virginia. We both enjoyed Dollywood. We especially loved the stage shows; they're always so much fun and so lighthearted. And Pastor Johnson appreciates the work they do at the bird sanctuary there. We were like two kids. We had a great time riding the train around the park, talking to the craftsmen at work." He wiped his brow with the back of his arm. "I've enjoyed the area, and it's nice to be living in Covington."

"Do you miss your congregation in South Carolina?" Grace asked.

Denny set the box cutter down. "Sometimes I do, but I find it challenging here. I enjoy a challenge and solving problems." He slapped his knee. "What do you say we call it a day? We've got another half-dozen or so boxes, and I'll handle them myself. You've given me enough of your time, and I thank you."

Happy to be done with the work, Grace closed the box she had just finished rummaging through. She took her time descending the narrow stairs, for they were not well lit and the handrail wobbled slightly beneath her hand.

Denny followed, dragging a box, thump, thump, behind him. "Thanks so much, Grace, for the cookies and coffee you brought. I'm going to take the cookies home to Pastor Johnson."

"Enjoy," she said, "and give him my very best."

Grace headed outside, followed by Denny, who dumped the box into the trash container at the side of the church.

4

Hands shoved deep into his jacket pockets, Pastor Ledbetter strode along Cove Road, turned left onto Elk Road, which was the main route out of Covington to Mars Hill, and walked toward Elk Plaza. There he bought a copy of the *Asheville Citizen Times* newspaper and sat on a bench in the shade to read it. Instead, he found himself people-watching. He recognized some of the folks in his congregation easily; others he was not sure of, so he nodded and smiled at everyone who passed by.

Alma Craine emerged from her car, her purse dangling over her shoulder. Her hair was sprayed stiff in an old-fashioned bouffant style. Firmly attached to her hand, her little granddaughter dragged her feet. Alma pulled the child across the parking lot while the little girl pointed toward the drugstore. Alma shook her head, turned toward the market, and noticed Denny on the bench. Looking flustered, as if she'd been caught with her hand in the till, Alma hastened toward him. The child pouted and half hid behind her grandmother.

"Howdy, Pastor," Alma said. "Such a nice day—enjoy it while you can. The weather's predicted to turn windy and cold, with rain by the weekend. It'll take all the leaves off the trees and ruin what's left of fall. That's what happened last year." She urged the impatient child from behind her. "Say hello to Pastor Denny, Mary Ellen."

The little face rounded Alma's hip. Two large blue eyes stared at him and her chin quivered. Denny expected her to wail, but instead the child stuck her thumb into her mouth and buried her face in her grandmother's thigh.

"I'll enjoy the fall while I can, and thank you for the weather update."

Because of the unsigned marriage certificates, he felt uncomfortable with her, especially as it had become clear to him that it was not his prerogative to continue to hide the information he'd stumbled upon. He had come to this decision in the wee hours of the morning, and had shared the entire matter with Pastor Johnson over breakfast. These couples needed to know their situation, even if it led to gossip and embarrassment. What mattered in the end was the legalization of their marriages.

As he watched Alma hustle her granddaughter into the market, Denny suddenly remembered that he had taken the letters back to his office and had left them on his desk, exposed for anyone who entered the office to see and read. He jumped to his feet. The newspaper hit the ground, and he did not stop to pick it up as he ran back to the church.

*   *   *

Charlie Herrill sat at Pastor Ledbetter's desk, reading one of the letters, his brow furrowed. He did not hear the door open and close, or the pastor's footsteps, nor did he see Denny until he cast a shadow across the desk.

Scowling, Charlie looked up. "I'm chairman of this congregation, and one of the couples affected by this business. Just when were you planning to show these to me? Or weren't you?" Charlie's voice was hard; his eyes reflected anger mixed with confusion and disbelief.

"As a matter of fact, this morning." Denny took the chair across from Charlie. "I found the folder with all that information yesterday." For a moment, only a moment, he was a small boy at the orphanage caught hoarding cookies, waiting to be punished. Then he straightened his shoulders. "Pastor Johnson is still the pastor here. I felt he should be apprised of the situation before I made my phone calls."

Charlie sighed and ran his fingers through his thick, graying hair. "Maybe it would have been better if you'd never opened that box, just dumped the whole bunch of crap in the trash." He tapped the letter on the desk. "Who else knows about this?"

"Grace Singleton. She helped me."

"She's sworn to secrecy, I assume."

"Yes." Suddenly Denny was alarmed. He hardly knew Grace. Was she trustworthy? "Is she someone who can keep a secret?"

"I believe she is," Charlie replied. "Better than many others I know." He cracked his big knuckles. "But how can you ever know? An unintended slip of the tongue, a revelation to one of her friends or her boyfriend, Bob. This stuff can do more harm than good, if it gets out in the wrong manner. Alma Craine's the biggest gossip in town, but this time the gossip would be about her." For a moment Charlie grinned, then he scowled. "And there's the moral and religious issues involved here. When a couple gets married in their church, they take vows that sanctify their marriage in the sight of God."

Charlie looked away from the pastor for a time, then nodded his head. "Tell you what, Pastor. My wife, Velma, is a sensible woman. I'll talk to her, and we'll figure something out. Alma is likely to get hysterical, and who knows about those McCorkle families and what they'll do. They're a tough bunch. A lot of them never got past high school, and they're quick with a fist."

"You're suggesting they'll come after me? I had nothing to do with it," Denny said, horrified.

"No, but you're the messenger. In the Greek myth, didn't they kill the messenger who brought the news of a lost battle? And at this point, we don't even know if those three McCorkle couples are still married or if any one of them has died or been divorced."

For a moment Denny visualized a horde of mean-looking men bearing down on him. Nonsense! He shook the thought away. He'd worked too hard over the years to gain self-confidence, to defend himself verbally, if not physically.

"I'm terribly sorry about this situation. Perhaps I

should have picked up the phone and called you the moment I discovered the contents of that correspondence, but it seemed appropriate to sleep on it and to discuss the matter with Pastor Johnson. If you find this unsuitable behavior and decide I am not the person you wish to hire when the time comes to replace Pastor Johnson, I will understand."

Charlie sat back. "Good Lord, nothing so drastic, Denny. The congregation likes you. I like you. I was spouting off. The shock of the thing, you know."

Denny nodded.

"You did exactly the right thing. It would have been disrespectful of Pastor Johnson had you not shared this with him and gotten his input. Now you and I will handle it together." Abruptly he stood. "Take your chair, Pastor. Let's figure out what's to be done. There's a reason for all this that only God understands, and it's not the end of the world, after all. Almost wants to make you laugh."

Relief swept over Denny. He rounded the desk, pulled the padded leather chair back to its original place, and slipped into it. He wore glasses, was not tall or tough, had never been muscular, or a fighter. In the orphanage they had bullied him, bruised him, and driven him to tears. It troubled him that after all these years, old anxieties, fears, and guilt could resurface at rare moments such as this. But he had left those papers on top of his desk, and that was tantamount to an invitation to anyone who entered to read them. Thank God it was Charlie and not anyone else who had happened upon them.

"There are four people who know about this," Charlie said. "Grace, Pastor Johnson, you, and I. Word will inevitably get out. That's the nature of the beast. After I discuss this with my wife and my lawyer, we'll have a meeting, you and I, Grace and Velma. Pastor Johnson also, if he's able. Grace is a sensible woman. People respect her. We'll make a plan, a possible way to cope with this information and the best way to present it to the others. But first, we have to find out exactly what is the status of our marriages in the eyes of the law."

"That's another problem. I called down to the courthouse at Marshall and spoke to the clerk of the court," Denny said. "I found out that in the state of North Carolina, common-law marriages are not legal."

"Common law's not legal in North Carolina? We've been together all these years and if one of us had died, the other would have found him or herself in a pickle. This gets worse by the second." He rose to leave. "You'll let Grace know that we're gonna have a meeting?"

Pastor Denny was glad to comply, relieved that the secrets were out and he had an ally in Charlie Herrell.

5

Later that afternoon, Charlie walked into the kitchen and asked Velma to take a ride with him.

"I'm ready to start canning. I've got this basket of late beans to deal with." She brushed back a strand of soft brown hair streaked with gray that had fallen onto her forehead, and looked up at him. Her eyes were hazel, large and bright.

"Leave the beans for later. I'll help you," Charlie said.

This sounded serious to Velma. Charlie seemed like a big, gruff man, but she knew that he was really a softy. However, stringing and cutting up beans and canning was hot, steamy work, and she could not recall his ever helping her. Velma slipped her red-and-white-striped apron over her head, folded it carefully, and laid it across a chair. She covered the basket of beans and set it far back on the counter. Their big, fat tabby cat, Olga, had been known to knock things off counters.

Charlie backed the pickup from their driveway and soon they were on the highway heading toward Asheville, then up onto the Blue Ridge Parkway. Neither had spoken, except for comments on the traffic.

"Why are we taking the parkway?" Velma asked.

"The leaves haven't all come off. I thought we could drive up to Pisgah Inn, have coffee or an early supper, if you'd like."

Velma's mind drifted back to her kitchen, and the beans, and the work ahead of her. "I'd just as soon not stop for supper." She found the out-of-state and local leaf watchers irritating, crawling along at twenty-five miles an hour. "Charlie, just pull the truck over at one of those lookouts. I don't have the patience for this today."

At the next lookout a car pulled out, and Charlie wedged the truck into the empty slot. Camera buffs were there in force, photographing the view.

"They're lucky today," Velma said. "It's so clear, they can shoot mountain ranges from here to Alabama." She preferred being in the valley, and felt safe and protected looking up at the mountains. This ocean of mountains that stretched to the horizon was another matter; the openness of this view turned her stomach queasy.

Velma studied Charlie's profile—his high forehead, his nose, grown nearer to his lips with age, it seemed. Had her nose grown? Removing her glasses, she ran her fingers along her nose, feeling the small bump that was generally concealed by her glasses. She cleaned them now with the tail of her shirt and put them back on. "What's this about, Charlie? Someone dead?

"No one's dead," he replied. "Just that things that you think are so, aren't."

"Like what things?"

Charlie rolled down his window. A fly zipped inside, buzzed about, and struck the windshield again and again in a frantic effort to get out. How many times could the fly strike the window without knocking itself out? Velma wondered. She thought of her daughter, Rosalie, who wanted a divorce so bad she could taste it, yet she couldn't make up her mind and do it. She just flailed about, beating her head against the wall of life, much like this fly against the window.

"Pastor Denny has been cleaning out the church attic with Grace's help," Charlie said.

"About time someone did," Velma replied.

"He found old bank statements and checks from the seventies and eighties."

"That long ago, and no one's dumped them?" Velma watched the fly perch on the edge of her closed window and wondered if it would linger long enough for her to wind the window down.

"Besides bank statements, he found letters and documents that go back forty years, long as we've been married." Charlie did not look at her, and his brow was furrowed.

"You brought me here to tell me this?" she asked impatiently.

"Now, hear me out, Velma." Charlie sighed deeply. "Remember Simms, the pastor who married us, the Craines, and a whole bunch of other folks?"

"I remember he left Covington in one big hurry. Never did know where he went or why."

"Turns out he wasn't a proper minister. He never graduated from that seminary in Ohio, like he said he did."

"How do you know all this?"

"It's in the papers Denny Ledbetter found. A letter from the seminary said Simms was kicked out before being ordained. He wasn't authorized to marry us or anyone else."

She gasped. "You're saying we're not legally married?"

"That's right." He grinned.

The whole thing *was* ludicrous. "You mean you're sitting next to your common-law wife?" She began to laugh. Why was such news so funny?

"We're not even that, honey. Seems North Carolina doesn't recognize common-law marriages."

Velma sobered. "You sure about this, Charlie?"

"Sure, I'm sure. Ledbetter's talked to them down at the courthouse."

"Who are the others? Us, the Craines, and who else? I can't rightly remember."

"Three McCorkle couples."

"Not married at all? What about our kids? What if one of us had died, Charlie?" She reached for his arm. "They're not dead, are they? I mean the McCorkles. They're all still together?"

"Pastor Johnson says they're all alive, and Denny's gonna check to see if they're all still living with each other. If they are, that would make five of us families still together, after so many years. Quite a record, I'd say."

"Lord, what will Alma do if she gets wind of this? So who knew about this back then? Who was the chairman of the church council, can you remember?"

"Griffen Anson. He's long passed on," Charlie said. "Lucky thing, too. One of those McCorkles might take a slug at him if he was still alive."

Velma scowled. "And you mean to say that Anson never told anyone? If we'd known, we could have just gone to the judge over in Marshall at the courthouse and gotten married legally. Who else knows about this?"

"Pastor Johnson and Grace. She was helping Denny clean out. I was thinking we ought to sit down with them and make a plan, before we tell the Craines and the Mc-Corkles. What do you think?"

"You're right, and there's only one plan I can think of: we've all got to get married, and soon!" Velma gasped, suddenly grasping the full implications of their situation. "What about our children?"

"Based on common law, they'd be legitimate, with this not being a common-law state, I don't reckon I know," Charlie said. "We have to talk to our lawyer."

Velma thought of their long life together. She had loved him in high school. When Charlie went into the army at eighteen, Velma, who was seventeen, cried herself to sleep many a night. After graduating high school she had worked part-time for her parents in their general store in Marshall, and lived for Charlie's letters, which were rare.

Charlie was one of the lucky ones. He made it home with only a shoulder wound that left his right arm weaker than the left, and precluded an anticipated career as a mechanic in his uncle's shop in Weaverville. They were married six months after he returned, and his folks helped them with the down payment on a small used mobile home, which they put on land just outside of Covington that belonged to Velma's grandmother Claudine.

Charlie's career path was for many years uncertain. He attended a technical school and became an audio technician for a local radio station, and later headed up the audio department. When a large out-of-town company bought the radio station, Charlie declined a promotion they offered him that included a move to Atlanta.

"I'm not leaving home," he announced to Velma, who was then pregnant with their daughter, Rosalie. The boys were toddlers.

Velma could not have been happier. She had no wish to separate from her mother and sisters, especially not to move to a big city.

Charlie then tried his hand at farming. "Figure I can handle plowing if I buy me a tractor," he'd said.

The tractor set them back all the money they had saved and cost them their first home, a small wooden house close to Weaverville, when that venture failed.

"Go to college," Velma urged. "Become a teacher. You'd be good teaching something technical. Maybe in electronics at one of the local colleges."

"You got to sit too much and think too much if you're a teacher," he'd replied. He'd tried his hand at selling tires at a friend's tire shop, and then for a short while sold encyclo-

pedias and hated that. In time, with Velma's encourage-
ment, he enrolled at the technical college and graduated as
a master electrician.

Herrill Electric started small, but grew slowly and steadily. Velma kept the books, sent out invoices, and collected
overdue bills. The business thrived and became well respected in Covington, Weaverville, Mars Hill, and as far
away as Black Mountain, where doing the wiring for a community center landed him larger and larger jobs: a hospital,
restaurants, apartment buildings.

After their children started high school, Velma, who had
never worked outside the home, grew restless. Visiting an
old aunt at a nursing home in Weaverville opened her eyes
to the loneliness of folks in nursing homes, especially those
who rarely had a visitor.

Nursing homes, she decided, revealed a lot about a person and how they had lived their life: whether they had
been an optimist or a pessimist, whether they had acquiesced to events or railed against them. One old woman
chose to sit in a chair in her room, made dark on a sunny
day by heavy drapes drawn against the light—so different
from the old man who led a line of wheelchairs along a cor-
ridor, singing all the way. Some days when she arrived at the
home, the faint odor of urine drifted through the corridors.
Other times it was the robust smell of Lysol or Pine-Sol.
Some days people seemed brighter, happier. They were glad
to see her, called her by name, and thanked her for coming.

Once a week at first, and then twice a week, Velma spent
several hours visiting men and women who had started out

as strangers and become family. She remembered their birthdays and brought gifts at Christmastime. When old Mrs. Grummund, to whom she had become especially attached, died at the age of ninety-four, Velma attended the funeral with Charlie.

"She was very old," he reminded her. "She had a good life, and more important, you were in her life these past few years. Your visits were a source of great joy for her, the manager of the home told me. She called you an angel from God."

Later, at home, Velma said, "I can't go on doing this. It hurts too much when someone I love dies."

"They love you at the nursing home. It's very special work you're doing there, honey. I'm right proud of you. Don't give it up."

Velma continued to visit people at the home, and she continued handling Charlie's books. They worked well together. They laughed together easily. When she lost her mother, Charlie was there to comfort and hold her.

"You got you a good man," said her father, who had once called Charlie a ne'er-do-well.

"I'm lucky," Velma replied. And she had occasion to say that over and over, like the time when Brad was eight and fell off a tree limb onto a picket fence post and rammed the spike into his groin. For a time it was touch-and-go while they waited to hear if Brad would lose a testicle. Charlie left his work to others and sat hour after hour with her in the waiting room.

"Brad's young and strong. He'll be all right."

"But what if they have to operate?"

"You can do fine with one testicle," he assured her.

She didn't believe he really knew that was true, but it comforted her, as did his big strong arms. Velma had cried and cried into his chest, soaking his shirt.

"What's a shirt," he said, and held her closer.

She cried again in relief when the doctor announced that no surgery was necessary. Velma was exhausted, and those first nights home, it was Charlie who stayed up with Brad. It had always been that way. Velma and Charlie faced and coped with life, illness, joys, births, and deaths together.

Velma now turned to look at her husband and felt her heart expand with love. "I love you, Charlie," she said. "Take me home to my beans, so I can get to work and start to think about all this. Do we want to just go down to the courthouse in Marshall, or maybe get married in church? You do want to marry me, don't you?" she teased.

"Well." He scratched his chin. "I'm thinking about it. I did see a cute young woman walking down the street in Mars Hill the other day."

She punched his arm, and he slipped his arm about her shoulder. "Seriously, whatever you want is fine with me, honey. I just want to make it legally right for us."

6

Although Denny had said that he would finish the attic himself, Grace felt she ought to give him any help he might need. The next day, Bob accompanied her to the church, ostensibly to help with the last few boxes. She hadn't invited him, but there he was bright and early, waiting on her porch. She suspected he'd do his utmost to get the "mystery in the attic" out of the attic.

Taking Grace's arm, he walked with her to the rear door of the church. She wanted to ask him to go away, but the door to the office swung open, and Pastor Ledbetter greeted them and welcomed Bob. With Bob there, Denny wouldn't be able to answer any of her questions about common law or anything else he might have found out. Sometimes Bob did things like this, which she considered pushy and inappropriate, and when he did, it annoyed her.

Denny seemed glad for their help, however, and the work went fast. Within an hour, what was left of sorting and rummaging in boxes was done, and the men carried the boxes down the stairs and out to the trash bin. The dust kicked up by the activity left them all sneezing.

As the men chatted, Denny asked Bob about his war experience.

"Thank God, I spent the Vietnam years in Germany, in ordnance," Bob said.

Ordnance, as Grace understood it, were all those things an army required to keep moving: guns, tanks, vehicles, oil, gas, and thousands of other items. Uninterested in hearing these details again, her mind wandered forward to Christmas.

Who was coming? Her son, Roger, homesteading in South Carolina, would probably come up. Bob, Russell and Emily, and the children. Russell and Emily had met and fallen in love on one of her visits to her parents, who had purchased one of the condominiums in Loring Valley. They had been married in a lovely ceremony in the ladies' backyard. Melissa had been born ten months later, and she and Tyler were as dear to Grace as any blood-kin grandchildren ever could be.

Hannah's daughters would certainly come for Christmas. Laura lived in Covington with her husband, Hank, and baby son, Andy; Miranda, her husband, Paul, and their two grown sons would drive down from Pennsylvania. Of course Mike would join them, as he did for all the holidays.

Bob, Max, Russell, and Tyler would pile into Max's pickup truck and drive to a Christmas tree farm in Yancey County, an hour away. They would walk in the field and after much deliberation and discussion they would select a tree. The owner of the tree farm would cut it and secure it in Max's truck, and home they would come. The tree would be beautiful, as it was every year, and almost touch the ceiling of the ladies' living room.

Once the tree was firmly in place everyone would help decorate it, each person adding their favorite ornaments, whether old and worn, homemade, or shiny new and store bought. This had become a tradition. The star was placed by the youngest member present, and last, to everyone's delight, the lights would be plugged in. Amelia and Mike would photograph the occasion.

They would buy a second tree, much smaller, to set up on the lawn in front of the house. Everyone did that on Cove Road, and the children had the grandest time decorating it.

Bob always made a bowl of his famous nonalcoholic eggnog the week before Christmas, and Grace would bake a stuffed turkey for the annual Christmas party in the church hall. She recalled hearing Velma and Alma speak about holding the party elsewhere this year, because the heat in the church wasn't reliable.

"And the church still stinks of smoke. It's all I can do to sit there Sunday mornings," Velma had said.

"We washed the pews and all with vinegar, but it's not done much good," Alma agreed.

"Wherever they have it this year, it's too much for you to bake a turkey for the church party and another one for Christmas dinner," Bob had stated. "I'm going to bring you a large spiral-cut Heavenly Ham for us to take to the church. It's easier to serve and less hassle for you, sweetheart."

"Let's call it a day," Denny said now, putting an end to Grace's musings.

Bob rose from his chair. "Now, Denny, anything else you need help with, just call me."

"Great," Denny replied, slapping Bob on the back.

7

꧁꧂

The meeting of the five couples had been called for two in the afternoon in the church hall. The McCorkles, whom Grace did not know, looked at her with a measure of suspicion when she arrived. Pastors Johnson and Ledbetter smiled at her and offered her a chair close by them. What must these people think? she wondered, as she studied their faces. Only the Herrills knew why they'd been asked to this meeting.

The Herrills and Craines smiled at her warmly, and Charlie introduced Grace to the McCorkles: Billy and May, Ralph and Bernice, June and Eddy. June was slim, with graying blond hair twisted in a bun at the back of her neck. May seemed a thinner, washed-out version of June, while Bernice's mouth was set in a thin line. Her permed hair had been dyed much too dark for her fair coloring.

The McCorkles cast anxious glances at one another. What had Charlie said to them when he'd phoned about this meeting? Grace considered herself an outsider in this matter, and though Charlie had said he wanted her unemotional opinion, she felt like an intruder and intended to stay as silent as possible.

The community hall was a large wood-paneled room with an unpolished wood floor. It was warm tonight, almost too warm, and Grace realized that she was not the only one feeling the heat.

The pastor wiped his brow. He stood and walked past the folding chairs stacked in towers along the wall, and tinkered with the controls for the heat. He shook his head. "The heat's not working right again. I can't get the temperature to stay the same from one half hour to the next. One minute it's too hot, then it's too cold." He crossed the room and sat down next to Grace.

A folding door separated the kitchen from the large open space. Ready at hand on a small table stood a coffeepot, paper cups, powdered creamer, and packets of non-sugar sweetener and real sugar.

"Help yourselves any time you'd like." Charlie waved his hand toward the coffeepot. "Velma makes a good cup of coffee."

"Let's get on with this, Charlie," Ralph McCorkle said. "I still got tobacco to get in before the day's out. There's a freeze predicted for tonight."

Bernice, Ralph's wife, poked at his arm. A buxom woman, she attempted to fan herself with a large plaid handkerchief. June McCorkle pushed back strands of damp hair. The McCorkle men sat stiffly, their backs flat against their chairs; they looked as if they would rather be anyplace else in the world.

Charlie cleared his throat. "I've asked you to come here this afternoon to share some information Pastor Denny came across while cleaning out our church attic. He's found some letters going back forty years to when that preacher, Simms, was here. Anyone remember that fellow?"

"Weren't that the minister who married us and then up and left?" Billy asked.

"That's the one. Grace, would you pass these letters around?" He handed her the photocopies he had made of the original letters.

"Now, let me explain," Charlie said. "To put it simply, Simms lied. He lied to old Griffen Anson, who was head of our council back then. Simms *wasn't* an ordained minister. Anson found him out when these letters came, and that's why Simms left. Anson didn't tell anyone, just shoved the letters in a box in the attic, and they've been there all this time."

Billy's eyes scrunched up as he studied the letter in his hand. He looked away, rubbed his eyes, and looked again. His lips moved slightly as he read the letter. Every now and then he glanced up at Charlie, the expression on his face a mix of disbelief and bewilderment.

June rummaged in her purse and fished out her husband's thick glasses, which he put on. Then he began to read the letter. Their expressions shifted and changed as they read. Eddy McCorkle flushed red. His brows knitted and June, apparently confused by what she was reading, looked at him as if for clarification.

Bernice's kerchief fluttered faster and faster, and her copy of the letter fell to the floor. She reached for it and looked as if she would topple from the chair. Her husband, Ralph, extended his hand to steady her. "Leave it be," he said.

Grace had never seen Ralph before. He was a burly, rough-looking man with a deeply lined face, probably from years of farming; a man decidedly more comfortable in his overalls than in the dress pants he now wore.

Billy concentrated on reading the letters. When he finished, his deep-set eyes fixed on Charlie. "Anson didn't tell nobody about this? I'd a liked to get my hands on him. I'd break his neck." Small whimpers issued from his wife, May, who appeared ready to burst into tears.

"What the letters mean," Pastor Ledbetter said, "is that none of you are legally married. Simms knew that, which is why he didn't turn in the marriage certificates to the courthouse. They were sitting in that box along with the letters to Anson."

"The son of a b . . ." Ralph's fists clenched.

"You're saying there ain't no record we was married?" June's fingers wrapped around Eddy's arm. Her face grew red and blotchy, her eyes wide and anxious.

Frank laid his copies of the letters in his lap and sat there stone-faced. Alma looked about her. "We're common-law married, though, right?"

Charlie raised his big hands. "Well, I thought so, too, and so did the pastor, here." He nodded toward Denny. "But it seems that North Carolina doesn't recognize common-law marriages."

"But we've been living together so long, we gotta be common-law married, and the kids legal," Ralph said. Disbelieving, he shook his head.

May began to cry softly. June, who sat alongside her—they were sisters, nonidentical twins, Grace later found out—took her hand. "It's okay, honey," June said. "We're bound to be legal somehow. That's right, ain't it, Mr. Herrill?"

Charlie shrugged. "I really don't know. My lawyer said he never heard of anything like this in all his days, and he'd have to look it up in his books. He did say the best thing we could do is to hurry up and get married. Only thing I'm sure of at this point is that we can't just go on as we are. We can't act as if Pastor Denny and Grace here, who was helping him clean the attic, never found any letters."

"Lord forgive us. All these years we've been livin' in sin." May's face looked like an apple that had had the skin rubbed off it. "What you think about that, June?"

Billy said, "I ain't never heard the likes of this." He stared at Charlie as if he were responsible for the whole darn mess. "You sure these here letters are true and real? Ain't some joke someone made up?"

"They're real, all right. I've got the originals." Charlie snapped open the briefcase on his lap and extracted the two yellowed sheets of paper.

Billy assumed the role of head honcho for the McCorkles. He strode over to Charlie, took the originals, and scowled down at them. "Well, I'll be doggoned." He returned to the circle and proceeded to show them to Ralph and Eddy and then to the women, who glanced at them briefly.

"They sure as heck look real," Eddy said.

"They're real, all right," Charlie said.

Body language, Grace believed, could tell you a lot about people. The McCorkle women, who were hearing all this for the first time and had had no time to consider any of it, appeared to be the most deeply affected. May and June drew their chairs closer and pressed against each other. Bernice bent slightly forward and held her stomach as if she had cramps. Alma pushed her chair back from Frank's, a trifle outside the circle. It was as if these women were unsure about their men or looked at them in a new light.

Grace wondered how she would have reacted if she and her deceased husband, Ted, had been called to such a meeting at their church back in Dentry, Ohio. Wouldn't she have been dismayed? Upset?

"I can marry any of you tomorrow and fix this whole thing," Pastor Denny was saying. "You wouldn't even have to go to a lawyer. You just have to go down to the courthouse and get a license, then I can marry you as quickly as you'd like."

"The courthouse? License? What we gonna say to Wanda Smith? She's the one gives out those licenses. She gave us the first one forty years ago. I can't go down there to her and do that again," Bernice said.

The women looked from one to the other.

"I don't much care who gives me a license. I don't know about the rest of you, but I'd sure feel a heck of a lot better if I went to my lawyer first and got his opinion," Frank said.

What would she and Ted have done in these circumstances? Grace wondered. Would they have run to the nearest church or courthouse and gotten married? Yes, she was sure they would have acted promptly and told no one.

Velma had had a few days to think about their dilemma. "We can't go on this way, that's certain. If any one of us passed away tomorrow, our family would have to hire plenty of lawyers to sort things out. I say we get married quick as we can."

Ralph's voice was husky. "What you think, Bernice?"

"Do we have to tell the children and grandkids?" Bernice shook her head. "I don't wanna tell 'em, Ralph."

"They'd probably laugh their heads off," he said.

"Any of us could get remarried in church, maybe a quiet little ceremony in the pastor's office, or just down to the courthouse," Charlie said. "Nobody's got to decide anything this minute, or even tomorrow, or the next day. We've all been together for over forty years, and we're darn lucky we're all alive and well and got each other, wouldn't you say?"

Heads nodded, except for May's, and Grace noted worried looks on everybody's faces.

Only Velma's face remained composed. "I know what Charlie and me got to do. I'd like to ask Pastor Ledbetter here to marry us as soon as possible. Charlie and me, we're gonna go down to the courthouse and get that license tomorrow—so if Wanda's still working there and she's snoopy and gossipy, she'll tell people."

Alma's head jerked in Velma's direction. "I think she's retired. I see her at the beauty parlor every so often. Whoever the new person is, whether she's a gossip or not, the word's still gonna get out and we'll be the laughingstocks of Covington."

"You and Frank could get married in another county. Maybe even drive on over to Wilmington, other side of the state, and do it," Velma replied. "But I agree with Alma: I just don't see how this is going to stay a secret. It's best if we have it out in the open."

Billy returned the letters to Charlie, who slipped them back into his briefcase. "Velma and I have had a day or two to think about this," Charlie said.

"Takes some thinking about, believe you me," Velma said.

"If we don't do or say anything, nobody's got to know nothing," Alma said, her voice pleading. "I feel right ashamed about this."

"Now, Alma, ain't nothing you've done to be ashamed of." Frank Craine turned to his wife. "There's all these people in this room who already know. How you gonna keep this a secret? You know we gotta get married, here or somewhere else."

Bernice glared at Alma. "I ain't no blabbermouth, like some folks."

"We're all in the same boat, Bernice." Ralph patted her arm.

Charlie looked directly at Alma. "I say we all go home and sleep on it. Way I see it, we've got options. Since we can't let it go like nothing's happened, we've got to either get married at the courthouse or have a church wedding, and do it right. Make a celebration of it, involve our kids and grandkids. We've got nothing to be ashamed of; it's not something we did wrong. It was a trick played on us by a lowdown, lying preacher. People will be sympathetic, is what I believe."

Alma shook her head. "I don't want nobody's pity."

"The way I see it," Velma said, "our friends and family will be as shocked and indignant about this as we are. Pity doesn't enter into this, Alma."

On that note, the meeting ended. The McCorkles left in a bunch, hardly taking time to say goodbye. Velma hooked her arm through Alma's and led her away. Their men drifted across the road to their homes. Grace and Pastor Denny added the chairs to a stack. Nobody had touched the coffee.

"Thank God we tackled the attic," Pastor Ledbetter said.

"I should have done it long ago," Pastor Johnson said. "These good people could have been in a lot of legal trouble, down the road. God bless you, Denny, my boy, and you too, Grace. I see the hand of God taking care of his own in this matter."

Grace unplugged the coffeepot and dumped the coffee in the sink. "Wouldn't it be nice if they all decided to get married in the church?"

"That would be nice, but look at it," Denny said. "It needs a good coat of paint and more scrubbing down. The pews need restaining. And sunlight doesn't make it through those lovely old stained-glass windows, with all the dust and grime covering them."

"Maybe we can do something about all that," Grace said.

8

It was early morning. The shadow cast by the ladies' farm-house draped across the front lawn almost to Cove Road. It fell across the cars parked on the gravel drive, across the bed of thickly mulched and pruned roses, and added to the chill of the day as Alma and Velma, bundled up in scarves and jackets, strode up to the house and climbed the steps of the front porch. Last night's frost had wilted the last of the purple verbena and salmon impatiens in Hannah's big clay pots, and the pots and rocking chairs had been pushed close to the house, out of the range of rain and snow.

Alma hesitated at the bottom of the porch steps. "It's a big favor to ask Grace, Amelia, and Hannah to do this for us."

"If we want to get married by Christmas, we've got to get them to help us. Remember how long it took to make Rosalie's wedding?"

"Almost a year," Alma said.

"If anyone knows how to do a wedding in a hurry, they do. Remember Miss Lurina's wedding, how she kept changing her mind about everything—the invitations, the dress, and all sorts of other things, like the date and the place—and then decided at the last minute? Grace made it all come out so nice."

Alma nodded. "Making that wedding happen would have tested the patience of Job." She recalled the time, years ago, when the ladies had invited them to a picnic, and she'd gone only because Frank had insisted. She'd felt very uncomfortable, sitting there with a heap of strangers under that old oak in their yard. But that was a long while ago, and she certainly didn't feel uncomfortable with Hannah or Grace any longer, especially not since the fire. Amelia? Well, Amelia was so different. Nothing bad to say about her, she was just different.

"Remember Lurina's pretty white satin gown? It was Grace who went to town and picked it out for her," Velma said. "Lurina trusted Grace. I trust her, too."

Alma still hesitated. "Shouldn't our families be doing this, instead of outsiders?"

"My boys sure aren't much good for this sort of thing. Are yours?"

Alma shrugged. "I only got daughters-in-law, so I never did put on a wedding, but you could ask Rosalie to help."

"Rosalie's got her own problems."

Velma reached out to ring the bell, but Alma's hand stopped her. "Wait a minute. Are we sure about this?"

"I'm sure," Velma said. "The more I think about it, the

more I like the idea. I thought you felt the same way."

"I don't know. Times are, I think it's okay, then I think it's just gonna make people talk more: sixtysome-year-old people getting married when they've lived together for forty years. Frank and I were planning another cruise to Mexico for our anniversary in November."

"Alma, we don't have a choice. And don't start with what people think or say; they're not the ones involved in this. It's not their lives or their children's. We decided."

"Well, it's not fixed in stone, is it?"

"No. You can change your mind and go stand up in some sterile courthouse and do whatever you want. But why not at least run it by Grace and Amelia? Amelia does flowers so pretty. Come on, now, Alma." Velma rang the bell.

Hannah opened the door. "Velma, Alma, what a nice surprise. Come in. Grace," she called over her shoulder. "We've got company."

Grace had just put two cupcake pans of healthy oatmeal-raisin muffins into the oven. Her cheek was smudged with whole wheat flour, as were her apron and hands up to her elbows. "Come on into the kitchen. It's nice and warm in here."

They followed Hannah into the large bright yellow kitchen with its octagonal alcove and round table.

"I like this arrangement," Velma said. "You don't have to be eating in the dining room all the time. Wish I'd thought about that when we were rebuilding our place after the fire."

"Our eating counter suits me and Frank fine," Alma

said. "Our kids don't eat at home much anymore. When they all come with the grandkids, we use the dining room."

The aroma of muffins baking filled the room, and they were well into their first cups of coffee before Velma stated the reason for their visit. "Alma and I have been talking. It might be right nice to ask the new pastor to marry us both in the church. A double wedding, I think they call it."

"Like a double wedding-ring quilt," Alma said. She was embarrassed, and her laugh was high-pitched and nervous. She patted her hair. Even at this early hour she was fully made up, cheeks rouged, lips glossed, eyes darkened with mascara, and she wore great hoop earrings.

"That would be so nice," Grace said. She thought of the list of things Denny had rattled off that needed doing to make the church presentable for weddings and for Christmas. A good coat of paint would help a lot, and could be done with the help of half a dozen volunteers. "I'm sure both pastors would be pleased," she said. "Is there some way I can help?"

Hannah, Velma noted, did not make the same offer or show any enthusiasm, and for a moment her spirits dampened. She focused her attention on Grace's smiling face. "We hoped you would help us organize it, get things in place so that they look pretty. Rosalie would help, but she's in such a mess what with wanting to divorce her husband and all, she can't think straight these days. Russell and Emily's wedding out in your garden was just so sweet, and I know you helped Miss Lurina with her wedding. I ran into

Miss Lurina yesterday over at the market and she was singing your praises. She says you're more of a daughter to her than any she could have had. You call her, and you go over, and you bring her food, and take her for outings. Poor thing's lookin' so frail and thin since Old Man passed. I told her what's happening with us, and she says to tell you she wants to help with our weddings if you'll help us. Just tell her what to do."

"I'm sure we can find a job for Miss Lurina," Grace said. "Have you talked to the pastor? Set a date? How many months do we have to plan this?"

"It smells like you better check the oven," Alma said. The aroma in the kitchen made all their mouths water.

"I'll do it, Grace." Hannah opened the oven, stuck a toothpick into the center of a fat muffin, and shook her head. "Couple more minutes."

"We'd like to marry just before Christmas," Velma said.

Alma nodded. "Christmas Eve afternoon. You reckon the Lord would think that was okay, it being the eve of His birthday and all?"

"Oh, my," Grace said. "He probably would be most pleased that you picked that day to celebrate something as special and happy as a wedding."

"You're talking weeks," Hannah said. "Weddings take months to organize."

"That's why we need your help," Velma said. "There's not been a wedding in our family since Rosalie married, and Alma's sons married in their wives' churches. You ladies know about weddings, about all the things that need doing."

"But just a few weeks . . . ," Grace said. "Can you get those muffins out of the oven for me, Hannah?"

Hannah removed the pan, shook out half a dozen muffins, and delivered them piping hot, along with butter, to the table.

"Try one," Grace said. "They're delicious and healthy, too. I use concentrated apple juice in place of sugar, and no white flour."

The few minutes it took to pass plates and to butter muffins gave them time to relax. Coffee cups were refilled.

"This is good," Alma said after eating the piece of muffin she'd slathered with butter. "Hot, but right good." She licked her fingers.

Velma cut her muffin into four neat pieces, and steam rose from all four sections. "Mercy me, they smell good," she said. "I think, with the short time and all, we could do it if you'd help us."

"Remember, there's Thanksgiving coming, and we'll all be making dinner for our families or going to visit family. We'll lose a couple of days right there. What do you think, Hannah? Can we organize two weddings in such a short time?" Grace asked.

"Not without Amelia. She's very creative. When you get her going, her mind spins off ideas faster than someone can spin wool into yarn," Hannah said. "But she's awfully busy these days, getting another photography book ready for the printer. That always takes so much time. I've seen it where Amelia thinks she's finished with a book, and the editor wants a different picture, then she's off shooting, sometimes for weeks, to get just the right one."

Velma looked worried. "But you'll at least ask Amelia?"

"Of course we will," Grace replied. "Weddings excite her, and hopefully she can enlist Mike's help. He's a genius with decorations and flowers."

"Well, first we got to ask Pastor Denny," Alma said. "But won't it hurt Pastor Johnson's feelings if we don't ask him to marry us?"

"Pastor Johnson thinks the world of Denny Ledbetter, and he trusts him. I think he wouldn't mind at all. He'd be proud of Denny," Grace said.

"I agree. He'll be delighted for his protégé," Velma said. "It'll be a big thing for him, his being so new and all."

Alma hesitated. "You don't think Pastor Johnson can do it?"

"He has trouble standing up without support. Reading the vows for two couples would probably be more than he could cope with," Velma said.

"You're right," Alma agreed. "I don't think he could do it. Pastor Denny, then."

"I agree," Grace said. She knew that the older man was relieved to have Denny Ledbetter lift any burden from his frail shoulders.

"If we do this, should we wear long white gowns? I don't think I want to do that, Velma. I'm too old for that." Alma looked almost petrified at the thought of a white gown.

"Goodness, no, Alma. We'd look ridiculous. I'm thinking a nice dress like you'd wear to go to somebody else's wedding, or a smart new suit."

"And no tuxedos. Frank won't put one of them things on his back. Says they're not good for anything but being buried in." Alma's tone was decisive.

"Just a nice suit. Not one that's been hanging in a closet for years and years," Velma said. "Getting Charlie out to buy one will be job enough."

"What have you gotten us into?" Hannah asked Grace after the women left, each taking several muffins for their husbands. "With all we have to do at Christmastime, you sign us on for two weddings? We haven't asked Amelia yet, either. What if she's too busy to help? And have you looked at the interior of that church? The outside's bad enough, but the inside stinks, and the fire smudged it all gray. I smell soot every time I go near the place."

"Charlie's the head of the church council; I'm sure he can get the church painted before Christmas. I'll talk to him. I'll get Bob, and you get Max to help. Charlie's sons could help, and Alma's, too."

Hannah leaned against the fridge with her arms crossed. "Ever think that there are no funds for painting, or they'd have done it long ago? The exterior of that church is a mess."

"What's a mess?" Amelia stood in the kitchen doorway. Her lovely white hair, usually so neatly pulled back from her face in a French twist, fell onto her forehead. She wore old, gray terry-cloth slippers and her well-worn blue fleece bathrobe, which matched the color of her eyes.

"You just missed Velma and Alma," Hannah said.

Amelia poured herself a cup of coffee and settled into a chair at the table. She yawned and shoved her hair back from her eyes. "What were they doing here this early?"

Grace explained the situation to Amelia. "They've decided to get remarried in church, and they want to do it on Christmas Eve."

Amelia bent over her coffee cup and inhaled its fragrance, as if the smell alone would wake her up. Her eyes widened in disbelief. "This is incredible. And they want a double wedding? In such a short time?"

"They came over to ask for our help planning the weddings. They probably can't put it together without us."

"And that's with everything: fixing up the church, the ceremony, the flowers, everything but selecting their wedding dresses," Hannah said. "I think they're in shock, after finding out they're not legally married."

"I'd be in shock, too," Grace said. "But it could be fun to roll up our sleeves and tackle these weddings. It would certainly add spice and excitement to the holidays."

"Fun, my eye," Hannah said. "It sounds like a lot of work to me."

"I like Velma and Alma so much better than I did at first," Grace replied. "When you get to know someone and understand about their lives, your feelings about them change. Don't you like them, Hannah?"

"I like them all right. I'm just not sure I want to take on their weddings. They're not my daughters and they're not even close friends."

Grace turned to Amelia. "Will you help? Would Mike

help with the decorations for the church, do you think? He's so incredibly good at that. You're both so creative. You could make it beautiful."

"Mike's taking people to the Florida Keys for a photography workshop in December. All that blue water and warm weather, while we're shivering here." Amelia shivered for effect, then went on. "I'll check the dates with him. Maybe he'll do it, if he's here."

She cut one of the two remaining muffins in half and buttered both halves. "So tell me about this wedding. Do both couples want to be married the same day, at the same time, or will there be one wedding and then the next? They're not going to stand in front of the minister together, are they?"

"I didn't get that impression. I think it's one after the other," Grace said.

"And are they going to wear white gowns at their age?" Amelia asked.

The three women spent the next half hour having their breakfast and discussing what it must be like discovering you weren't married after forty years.

"I'd want to run away," Amelia said.

"I'd probably ignore the whole thing," was Hannah's judgment, while Grace loved the idea of weddings.

"I'd do exactly as Alma and Velma are. I wonder what the McCorkle families are going to do? Now, they're an odd bunch. I get the sense they don't like Velma and Alma, and don't trust anyone but one another."

"So what's new? That's the McCorkles," Amelia said.

*   *   *

For the McCorkle women, it had been difficult to even talk about the situation with their hardheaded men.

"I said, Eddy, let's go on down to the courthouse, get married real quick, and make the thing right. But you know him, he can get real stubborn," June told her sister. "He said we've been living like this all these years, so what's the difference? It's like he doesn't want to think that we're not even considered common-law married. But I think it's kind of romantic getting married again, like starting over."

"I wish nobody had ever told us about it," May replied. The prospect of remarrying Billy revolted her. Whenever she looked at her husband, her heart sank and she wanted to cry. She didn't like being married to him, hadn't for more years than she could remember, and didn't want to be remarrying him. She had been seventeen years old and had gotten pregnant after one foolish summer night down by the river, following a school dance. No one knew, though some might have suspected the truth when she delivered their first child two months early.

She had to give Billy credit for marrying her. He could have said he didn't have a thing to do with making the baby. At the time she'd been thankful and relieved, yet at the same time she'd felt trapped, as she was sure Billy also felt. He'd get this faraway look in his eyes and change the subject whenever she had talked about the coming baby. He didn't want to feel it kick, and he hardly paid no mind to Tucker after he was born or anytime since.

All these years, and they had never talked about their

real feelings with each other or anyone else. She had been too ashamed to tell June, who was so happy with Eddy. May and Billy hardly spoke about anything, except maybe the tobacco crop spoiling or being a good one, or when she needed him to help correct one of the children. Mainly he worked, ate, and watched television.

She'd never worked outside the home and focused her life on cooking, cleaning, raising children, which took much of her energy, and trying her best to avoid her mother, Ida, who loved Billy and loved coming over for a meal or just to sit and drink beer with him and watch a ball game. May hated how loud they turned up the television. It seemed to her, looking back at her life with her husband, that it was one long stupid mistake.

For a while they'd had the sex thing. They had four kids to show for that. But then the passion went, leaving absolutely nothing. Many a night, after Billy fell asleep, May would sit in the living room and cry softly. Billy wasn't a good and caring man like Eddy. He wasn't kindhearted or generous. He'd throw his dirty clothes on the bed, so she'd have to wash the heavy bedspread nearly every other day to keep it smelling fresh. He tracked mud in after every rain and grass after each mowing.

Oh, she could go on and on about the things he did that made life harder for her. If she had gone to school and learned a trade, she would have left him long ago. Instead she was trapped, and it was slowly but surely taking the very life out of her. Marry Billy again? "Oh, dear God," she prayed, "show me a way out of having to do that."

May would have told June many times how she felt, but June was forever relating some grand thing Eddy had done, like telling her how pretty she was, or buying her a gift, a pair of earrings or a nice warm scarf, or planning a trip to Walt Disney World or Dollywood with their kids. And now June was so excited at the prospect of remarrying Eddy. May figured she'd best keep her thoughts to herself, as she'd done these forty years.

For years the sisters had done their laundry together, one week at June's, the following week at May's home. They lived two doors from each other, and it was a lot easier folding king-sized sheets with another person. Their laundry days also gave them a chance to visit and catch up on local gossip and to talk about their concerns, mostly about their children. They had eight between them, plus grandkids, and it was always something. Sometimes days or weeks passed without private moments when they could be alone, for June worked part-time keeping books for Lily's Beauty Salon on Elk Road, and their mother, Ida, popped in whenever she chose, with never a phone call or a by-your-leave.

"Mary Alice is the only one of my kids that got upset when I told 'em," May said. "Tucker, Joey, and Susie thought it was funny. Sundays, when they come for supper, they go on and on making jokes about Billy and me livin' in sin and them being illegitimate, like it was something to be proud of. Last Sunday Billy got real mad. He slammed the table with his fist so hard he spilled his soup on the floor. Now, that was a mess to clean up, all them vegetables and noodles."

"I'm mad, too, but not at my kids. Every time I think of old Anson not telling anyone, not having any thought for what might happen to us down the road, I see red. For the first time ever, I'm glad my girls live down in Atlanta and over in Athens, and not under my nose making remarks like that." June pulled a sheet from the dryer. It was tangled around another sheet and had to be untwisted to straighten it out. When she finally freed it, she held a section out to her sister. "Seriously, May, what are we gonna do? Knowing what we know now, we can't just leave it like it is, can we?"

May did not reply. She moved away, straightening the sheet as she went, and they folded it again and then again into a nice parcel fit for shelving.

"Velma and Alma are going to get married in church Christmas Eve. Ma told me," June said. She'd given the matter a lot of thought, lying awake nights thinking about it. "We might could do it in church, too, over the holidays, or next year, or we could do it simple and quiet like, maybe even at home. I think the minister would come to the house under the circumstances. And then we wouldn't have to tell a soul. But we'd be right with God, and that's what counts."

Still May said nothing.

June persisted. "We've got to do it together. Billy and Eddy won't agree unless the other one does. Mama's gonna put pressure on them."

May turned away and began to fold pillowcases. She didn't want June to see the pain in her eyes, and it puzzled her now, as it had many times, that June couldn't feel her distress. Couldn't June hear how gruffly Billy spoke to her? See how demanding and controlling he was? Didn't her sister know how unhappy she had been?

But then, why was she blaming June? Perhaps she had kept the secret from June for fear that if she said something, it would be like a dam breaking apart, and she'd be swept away, destroyed.

9

Denny Ledbetter leaned over his computer. It had been a farewell gift from his congregation in South Carolina, and he had mastered the word processing program and no longer typed with one finger. Today he must focus on typing Sunday's sermon. What with those two weddings pending, somehow he had to tie the Lord into an appeal for funds to paint the interior of the church.

He'd been over and over the books with Miss Pratt, the bookkeeper who'd kept Cove Road Church's books for years. Nothing about her inspired his confidence. She worked from home in cramped quarters and kept the books by hand, without the assistance of an adding machine. He'd watched her dampen her pencil on her tongue before starting to add a column of figures. Did she even know about new tax laws, possible new deductions available to churches, and so on? One thing she was adamant about, "There's nary a penny for paint and labor."

He had looked at her and wondered what her life had been like. She appeared every bit the stereotypical spinster: graying hair fastened tight in a bun, faded brown eyes behind thick glasses, a long shapeless sweater over a shapeless blouse and skirt, Buster Brown–type shoes with laces.

"We're paying you more than we ever paid Pastor Johnson," she had informed him. "It's cleaned out our treasury." She seemed huffy and downright unfriendly, and he'd been glad to close her door behind him. *Poor Pastor Johnson. How had the old man managed?*

"She's honest as the day is long," Charlie had said, when Denny asked about Miss Pratt.

Though Miss Pratt had taken delight in letting him know that he was overpaid by her standards, Denny had taken a cut in salary to come to Covington. He sat at his desk, planted his elbows firmly on the smooth surface, and rested his head in his hands. Right off, he had gotten himself into this mess about the marriages. He felt as if everyone blamed him, including Miss Pratt, and especially the McCorkles.

And now the Herrills and Craines wanted to have a double wedding on the afternoon of Christmas Eve. The walls and pews and floor of the church had absorbed so much smoke from that fire a couple of years ago that they'd never let go of it. The walls needed a good coat of paint. The pews and floor needed washing down again. And the old boiler was either too hot or not hot enough. Coughing and clunking, it was ready to die any minute, and there were no funds to replace it. "Without heat, the church will be too cold for Christmas service, let alone two weddings," Denny said aloud, startling himself.

Looking up at the plain wooden cross on the wall, Denny wondered what Jesus would say to this congregation if he were their pastor. Jesus had multiplied the loaves and the fishes, but how in heaven could he, a humble minister, multiply the two cans of paint that he could afford to contribute into the twenty needed to paint the interior of the church? And there was that rotting floorboard he avoided every time he walked across to the pulpit, and the step that wobbled whenever he stepped on it, and heaven only knew what else needed repairs. It seemed that he found another problem every day. What had Pastor Johnson done about all these things? Maybe he had grown discouraged about the lack of funds and simply overlooked them.

Grace poked her head into Denny's office. "Busy, Pastor?"

"Worried, not busy," he replied, looking up at her. She was the epitome of what he imagined a loving mother or grandmother would be: warm, caring, sympathetic, and encouraging. She was like the mother he had ached for and had never known.

"Tell me what's worrying you." Grace sat across from him, her face kind, her brown eyes interested and hopeful. He felt more cheerful just looking at this pleasingly plump little woman. In his mind, he called her Granny Grace.

"The church needs painting. The boiler is on its last legs.

There's a rotten board near the pulpit, and the steps to the pulpit need fixing. Miss Pratt has declared that there's no money in the treasury."

"Well, let's put our heads together and try to solve the problem. For starters, it's manpower and paint that's needed. A floorboard here and there can't be hard to repair, and one of Charlie's sons is a carpenter. I believe we can get everything we need donated—except a new furnace, of course. We'll need cash to replace that if it goes."

"When it goes."

"When it goes. Look at you, your face is as pale as if you were a mole in a hole, and you've got dark circles under your eyes. If I may say so, you need a couple of good nights' sleep and some sunshine, Pastor. Do you go walking or running, maybe? Looks to me like you need to get out in the fresh air."

"I try to do a bit of walking."

"You haven't had breakfast, I bet."

He hadn't.

Grace held out a bag to him. "Healthy muffins, baked fresh this morning. I make them every three or four days; everyone likes them. Max and Bob drop in almost every day for coffee and muffins. Oats and bran lower choles-terol. I make them as much for Bob as for myself. He has high cholesterol, you know, and he's been working with his doctor to find a medication that he can tolerate. He's tried Lipitor and Zocor without luck. He got dizzy with the one and muscle cramps in his legs when he took the other. We're trying a dietary approach before Bob goes on yet another drug." Grace handed Denny the muffins. "Lordy, I'm rattling on."

"You're very kind, Grace, and you're not even a member of the congregation. Do you belong to another church?"

"No. You could say I'm nondenominational, even ecumenical." She tapped her chest. "God lives inside of me, that is what I've come to believe." Once, on a cruise ship in the Caribbean, out of the blue she had had a spiritual experience. She hadn't been praying or meditating; she'd been drinking in the beauty of nature, and had felt a sense of being at one with the universe. She had been enveloped in a cocoon of love so deep and so abiding, that she had never been able to put her feelings and the wonder of it into words.

"You're not a church member, yet you do so much for me and for Pastor Johnson. He told me."

"We're neighbors. Pastor Johnson is a very good man and you're a good man, Denny Ledbetter. I come to church out of respect for special occasions, mostly holidays and weddings. God is everywhere."

"I understand how you feel, and I appreciate your help, Grace." He broke a muffin in two and began to eat. "This is wonderful. How can it taste so good and be healthy, too?"

"The secret's apple juice concentrate and grated apples, I think," she replied. "Helps to hold the moisture. Do you have a coffeepot in here? I'll make some coffee."

Denny showed her where the supplies were, and as she brewed a pot, he began to relax. "It's very different here.

Down in South Carolina I'd meet with the church council, tell them what was needed, and they'd take on the project. The women's auxiliary ran bake sales, raffles, and craft fairs. The year before I left, they started doing silent auctions. That really raised money."

"You could try to organize a woman's auxiliary."

"When I suggested it, the council members discouraged me. They said the younger women work outside the home, and many of the older women help them by taking care of their kids. Our congregation's too small for an auxiliary, they feel."

"It's not a matter of size. It's a matter of will and enthusiasm," Grace said.

Just what he'd expect from this terrific lady. "You're right, Grace. Can you suggest someone you think has those attributes, the will and enthusiasm?"

She handed him a cup of coffee. "I have to think about it. I've got to go now, but I'll get back to you."

"Thanks, you've made me feel better. Now I can get on with writing this sermon." When she closed the door behind her, he began to type, and this time the words flowed.

"Now, just who do you think has an interest in starting an auxiliary, or even taking on a fund-raising project?" Hannah asked. "The council's right. Most of the young women work. A lot of the older women spend their time helping their daughters and daughters-in-law by driving grandkids to ball practice, karate, or dance lessons, or they're lugging their grandbabies to the market with them."

Grace recalled that last winter she'd watched from her kitchen window as red-cheeked, red-jacketed youngsters careened down the hillside across the road on the lids of trash cans. She thought of those children throwing snowballs at one another, giggling, yelling, and having fun. They were all someone's grandchildren, but mainly Velma's and Alma's. And yet Alma had time to sit for two hours each week at the beauty parlor, and Velma had time to help at a nursing home in Weaverville.

"Let's invite the five women getting married for dessert one evening after supper. We'll tell each of them to bring another family member, a mother, aunt, sister, or a daughter. With a group of women like that, we're bound to come up with great ideas," Grace said. *That's the beauty of women. We multitask. We see the big picture.*

Hannah acquiesced without even a sigh. "I'll ask Laura. My daughter would benefit from expanding her interests in the community a bit, and we'll ask Brenda and her daughter, Molly. That should give us a nice pool of women."

"And Lurina. We can't leave her out. I'm going to go see her and tell her what's going on. She'll get a kick out of this business," Grace said.

They decided that personal phone invitations would be best, and Hannah agreed to make the calls from her office.

"Have you heard," Hannah asked June, "that the Herrills and Craines plan to be married Christmas Eve in the church?" A pause. "No, not during the service, the ceremony will be at two in the afternoon, so as not to conflict with the Christmas Eve service."

"I cannot believe anyone would want to get married in that stinky old place," June replied.

"I guess smoke from the fire wormed its way into everything: walls, pews, floor, didn't it?" Hannah said. "I understand the ladies of the church washed the pews down with vinegar."

"We worked like dogs, and it didn't help much," June said.

"Maybe it can't be done with only one washing. Look how long it took for the smell to go out of the air after the fire. We could smell it up in Loring Valley, where we stayed afterward."

"You're right. We could smell it all the way into Mc-Corkle Creek," June said.

With every call, I'm getting better at this, Hannah thought. Grace had done it again, gotten her involved, and she was actually enthusiastic over something she hadn't given a hoot about. It had become a challenge to see if she could involve the other women, to win them over, so to speak.

"Anyhow," Hannah continued, "you know how it is. We women see things men don't. We're the ones who get things done in the community, at home, with our kids. Maybe we could come together, we women, and talk about this whole situation. We'd like it if you'd drop by next Tuesday evening after supper. Grace is making some delicious desserts. Come have some with us, say about eight. Is that a good time for you?"

June sounded surprised. "Oh!" She hesitated a moment. "Well, don't that sound mighty fine."

"And bring another woman along—your mother, or your aunt, or a cousin—and of course May's invited. I'm going to call her, and then Bernice, the minute I hang up from you."

Sounding pleased, June accepted.

10

⚜

Resilient as ever, tough-minded and straight speaking, eighty-four-year-old Lurina Masterson Reynolds reached up on her toes and gave Grace a big, affectionate hug. "You been busy, Grace? I heard you been cleaning out the church attic with the new minister. You like him? He's awful young, I heard."

"He's about thirty. He had his own congregation down in South Carolina for six years. You're just used to a much older minister."

"Well, he ain't been to call on me yet. Pastor Johnson used to come by every week, snow, rain, or shine."

"Denny Ledbetter's his name," Grace replied. "And I think you'll like him. He's only been here a short time, and it seems like everything's come down on his head. It looks as if Pastor Johnson let things slip pretty badly these last few years."

"Remember how spry Pastor Johnson was, playing the

banjo like he did, and everyone singing along last summer when you all had that neighborhood party over on your road?"

"Yes. But afterward he just about collapsed, when Charlie helped him down from the platform."

Lurina nodded. "That's true. He sure didn't look spry then."

"The new minister hasn't had time to catch his breath yet. It was suggested that he clean out the church attic, which hadn't been touched for forty years or more. That's why I offered to help him. The poor fellow is just getting to know who belongs to the church, and whom he ought to be visiting. He'll catch on to it all in good time."

"How come you know him so good?"

"I've been taking Pastor Johnson cookies, cake, or a pot of stew each week for a while. I went over with cookies the other day, and I met Denny Ledbetter in the graveyard on my way to the house. He'd been cleaning up around those graves no one ever tends. He's adopted some of the dead people and takes care of their graves as if they were his family. He says he does that because he was an orphan and grew up in an orphanage and doesn't know any family."

"He sounds like he might be a good fellow. But adopting dead folks? That sounds like he's slightly tetched." Lurina tapped both sides of her head with her fingers. Her free laughter rang out like jingling bells, and Grace laughed with her.

"Denny will be visiting you soon," Grace said.

Lurina stepped back and placed her hands on her hips.

Grace was not tall, but the top of Lurina's head reached only to her chin. When Lurina smiled or laughed, her blue eyes vanished amid the folds in her small, wrinkled face. She loved teasing Grace.

"You tell him he better get himself over here, or I'll take my shotgun and come lookin' for him."

Lurina's shotgun was a source of much amused discussion around Covington. Sometimes, weather permitting, she sat out on her porch in a rocking chair that groaned when it moved, as if it, too, had arthritis, with the old double barrel across her lap. Only to Grace had she ever admitted that there was no shot in the shotgun and, in fact, she didn't even know how to load or shoot it. In the house, she kept it stashed with the umbrellas in the umbrella stand.

Lurina stopped laughing, and her face grew sad. "I sure do miss Joseph Elisha. Funny, ain't it? Eighty-one years, I lived alone. Then for three short years I was married up with Joseph Elisha, and with him gone the place seems so big I can't find nowhere to sit and be at peace."

"He was a good man," Grace said. Joseph Elisha had been known to everyone as Old Man. Since he had died, Grace worried about Lurina living alone in this big, drafty house. But Lurina would not hear of moving. Besides, there were Old Man's pigs in the pen out back to be cared for.

Lurina began to wring her hands. "Wayne came by the other day and took off a whole heap of pigs. He says that's what his grandpa said he should do, sell 'em and give me the money. But to tell you the truth, Grace, I don't need no money, and them pigs are all I got left of Joseph Elisha. I get up in the morning knowing I got to get out there and feed them. Some days I stand at my kitchen window and talk to them, and when I talk to them close up, I swear that fat sow, Lolly, grunts back to me like she knows what I'm saying."

"Wayne didn't take Lolly, did he?"

"You think I'd let him?" Lurina shook her head, and her thin white hair flew about her face. "He left Lolly and a couple of other sows, Mattie and Little Sue. They're gonna drop babies any day now. And he left a big old male I call Buddy, and a couple of medium-sized sows that ain't got no names, who weren't fat enough for market."

"You may have fewer pigs now, but every one of them needs you to get up and feed them every day," Grace said.

She thought goats were valuable, for they kept the grass cropped, as if by a lawn mower; and sheep were sweet looking, and soft to touch, and their wool made warm coats and sweaters. Deer, with their lovely eyes and sleek bodies, thrilled her, and on the rare occasion that a deer felt safe enough to venture into their backyard and she saw it, Grace would sit silent, transfixed, wishing she could talk to it and that it could understand her.

But pigs? She'd heard they were intelligent, but they were so, well, ugly. She respected Lurina's affection for them, though, and Old Man had certainly loved his pigs. When he'd married Lurina, a special pen had had to be built on her property, and he brought every last one of his pigs down from his home in the mountains up near Tennessee.

Lurina and Grace moved into the kitchen at the rear of the old farmhouse. Lurina poured them each a glass of orange juice, then pulled out a chair and joined her at the old table.

Grace spent the next half hour telling Lurina all the news about Griffen Anson hiding the letters, about Simms never being ordained, and about North Carolina not being a common-law state. "I'm sure if their property is in both their names, there'd be no problem, but how it affects their children's inheritance, I couldn't guess," she said.

At the name Griffen Anson, Lurina knitted her brows. "I knew that man. Nothin' nice about him. He was so stingy, he'd skin a flea for its hide. He cheated my pa once in a card game and Pa never forgot. Pa and I never went to that funeral when Anson passed. Anson never cared about nobody. He hid those unsigned marriage certificates 'cause he didn't want anyone to know he got fooled by that fellow Simms, and that he didn't check the records on him properly.

"I went to church one time with Pa when Simms first came. Pa wanted to hear what kinda preacher he was. We ain't never went back to church while he was here. Pa said that fellow Simms was slick as a greased pig."

"He surely was," Grace agreed. "And all these years later, we have five couples coping with the shock that they are not legally married, and that they don't even have the comfort of common law to fall back on."

"And now they're gonna get themselves married in church." Lurina laughed. "They're sure gonna look silly, women in their sixties parading down the aisle like young fillies."

"Not if we plan a dignified affair. Not if people understand what's at stake here. Will you help us?"

"Sure! What you want me to do?"

"Well, for one thing, help me pass the dessert when I have the women over for planning meetings. Hannah's organizing the ceremonies at the church, and she could use some help with the details. Maybe you can help Mike and Amelia with the flowers, and just your being there will help. You got married to Old Man at the ripe old age of eighty-one. These women all respect you, and I think it would mean a lot if you would encourage them. They're afraid of looking ridiculous."

Lurina cleared her throat and placed her palms flat on the table. "I see your point. No sense making them feel worse than they do. Sounds like things I could manage, Grace, my girl. You need me, I'll be there."

"We're having the women over for dessert soon. Bob or I will come pick you up. It could run late, so plan on sleeping over that night, okay?"

"Sure. I like staying over in your guest room. I get to lie in bed and watch television, and just being in a different house makes it feel special. And I get tea in bed. You treat me real good, Grace, and I appreciate it. I hope you know that."

"It's a pleasure to have you," Grace said.

Lurina's nose crinkled. "You having those McCorkles to your house?"

"Yes, of course. They're among the five couples. June and May are nice, quiet women, and Bernice"—Grace wiggled her hand in the air—"she's tougher, but you get used to her. She's quite heavy. Buxom, Hannah calls it. Seems to me she doesn't feel comfortable in her body." She laughed. "But who am I to criticize anyone for being overweight? I think Bernice is probably self-conscious about how she looks, and she's snippy sometimes."

"Snip at me and she'll get the back of my hand," Lurina said.

Grace smiled, picturing little Lurina backhanding Bernice, who could swat Lurina against a wall like a fly. But of course, Bernice would never be anything but respectful of Lurina's advanced age, and they would all treat her kindly and with deference.

11

On the night of the dessert meeting, Max and Bob had brought over folding chairs from the church for the group that gathered in the ladies' living room. The gas fireplace glowed, warming the room and making it cozy and pleasant. Some of the women noticed Amelia's photographs over the fireplace and commented on how nice they were.

"I recognize that creek," June said, pulling her sister over to look at the photograph. "Remember, May, we used to swim in Jetter's Creek."

"How can you recognize it?" May asked.

"Those boulders. Ain't no creek around here with big, round boulders like that but Jetter's Creek." She turned toward Amelia. "Ain't it Jetter's Creek?"

Amelia confirmed that it was, indeed. "It was a long walk from where I parked the car, if I remember right."

May nodded. "It sure was a far piece from the road. Mostly I remember how cold the water was, even in summer." She hugged her shoulders as if to ward off the memory of the cold. "I couldn't get warm nohow afterward."

As everyone gathered at the buffet table, Grace encouraged them to try both the orange pound cake garnished with peaches and cream, and the chocolate mousse cake. Lurina helped with the tea and coffee. She wore a long print dress that she kept for special occasions in a mothball-saturated closet, and the dress, although it had been hung out to air for a day, retained the faint odor of mothballs.

"This is good and fancy," June proclaimed after taking her first bite of chocolate cake. "Strange name for it, though. Mousse, like that hair stuff."

"It's a French word," Amelia said. "Actually, it means 'foam' or 'froth.' When you make a mousse, you whip up ingredients and they get light and frothy."

"Like the way that hair stuff comes out in your hand, as if it'd been whipped with an egg beater," June said.

Before the evening was out, several women asked Grace for her recipes. She should publish a recipe book, they said.

When everyone had eaten and the dishes had been removed, Velma addressed them. "I want to thank Grace for her great desserts." She patted her stomach. "Worth every pound, wouldn't you say?"

Everyone smiled and nodded.

"It was good of you all to come," Velma continued. "This meeting's about us and about Simms and what he did to us all, and about how we women can get to work and clean up his mess."

"In the old times he'd of have been caught up with, tarred and feathered," Betty, Bernice's grandmother, who looked a hundred, said.

"Imagine if Pastor Denny hadn't cleaned out the attic," Velma said. "We'd have gone to our graves without the proper marriage in God's eyes, and the Lord only knows what kind of problems there'd be for our kids and grand-kids afterward."

"You got that right," Alma said. "My kids joke about the situation, but it wouldn't be so funny if we was gone and they had to hire lawyers to set the whole thing right. Could take years."

Gray, brown, blond, and white heads bobbed up and down in agreement.

"But ladies," Velma said, "this meeting's not just about us couples thinking we were married. After the fire, everyone on the church's side of the road repainted their houses in-side and out. Maxwell did, and the Tates and the Lunds, and the office at Bella's Park, too, which didn't even get the worst of it. Every house, every barn, and every building, ex-cept for our church, got a fresh coat of paint. And we've all—including me and Alma, whose houses burned—sat in that church week after week, and complained about headaches, or how our eyes burned. Even when we left the church feel-ing sick from the smell of smoke, we didn't lift a finger to do a thing about it."

Agreement again, and they looked at one another with a sense of surprise that, as members of the congregation, they hadn't "lifted a finger" to do a thing about it.

"The men haven't complained. They're probably scared we'd ask them to paint the place," said Ida, a large, raw-boned woman. June and May's mother, she was as different from her daughters as broccoli from beets, and had strong opinions about everything.

"And that is exactly what we need for them to do," Velma said. "We need them to roll up their sleeves and pitch in and get the place painted before Christmas."

"You got to be joking," Ida said. "They'd as soon cut to-bacco all day long in hundred-degree weather as pick up a paintbrush."

"Or putter all week fixing a tractor or a truck," another woman said.

"Or tend their pigs," Lurina added.

"Painting is sissy work, far as they're concerned," Ida said.

The women sat in silence for a few moments.

"There's something else," Velma said. "Alma and I'd like to invite you, May, June, and Bernice, to be married in the church on the afternoon of Christmas Eve, too. All of us together."

Someone giggled.

"A wedding for five couples?" Bernice appeared put off by that idea. "How in the world are we gonna do that? Who goes first, and who goes last?"

"We could draw lots to see who goes first, second, and so on," Alma said.

Bernice scowled. "I don't know about that."

June gave her a good hard look. "I like the idea. It's

never been done around here. It's something nice everyone will talk about, and our kids will remember. It's a lot better than standing up plain like in the courthouse. Anyone could do that."

"It's not something you have to decide today," Velma said. "But either way, we sure do need to get some folks interested in donating paint and volunteering to help paint the inside of our church before Christmas Eve, wouldn't you say?"

"My Ralph never painted nothin' in his whole life," Bernice said. "Stubborn as he is, he ain't gonna start now."

"Well then, he won't. A few men can handle the job, especially if those who don't paint will bring ladders or drop cloths, or donate the paint or brushes." Velma was not about to give up.

"Will it affect who goes first down the aisle? Who paints, I mean," Bernice asked.

"Heavens to Betsy, Bernice. The painting won't affect anything but the painting," June said. "I promise you, if we all do decide to get married together and you get last place, I'll change places with you. I don't care when I walk down the aisle, just so's I get married proper."

"What about having a matron of honor?" Bernice asked.

"And flower girls?" May asked sarcastically.

Grace jumped in. "Why not? It's your wedding. You should be able to do whatever you want."

"What about Christmas Eve service?" Ida asked.

Velma answered, "Pastor Ledbetter says he'll do it after the weddings are done."

"He could have Christmas Eve service the night of the twenty-third," June suggested.

"That would be mighty peculiar," said Bernice. "Seems to me Christmas Eve is Christmas Eve, not the day before."

"It'll have to be a very short service if we're gonna stay for it. With all our friends and family here, we'd be having a little reception back at the house," Alma said.

"Maybe he could do a service first and we can be married after, if we decide to do it then," June said.

"All of that can be decided later," Velma said.

"I think it would be fun getting married, all of us, the same day." Alma was past objecting. Velma had taken her for lunch in Weaverville at the Sunnyside Café and plied her with sweet tea and pastries, and teased her with the prospect of shopping for the perfect wedding dress. In the end, Alma had agreed and plunged wholeheartedly into the idea. "Mature women like us can bring so much more style to a wedding than a young girl can. And we won't be nervous, shaking in our shoes this time."

"Did you shake in your shoes, walkin' down that aisle, when you married Frank, Alma?" June asked.

"I was shaking like a wet cat," Alma said. "Until I started down the aisle, anyway. Then I got real bold. I liked it when folks all stood up and turned around to look at me. Made me feel real special. We had a big wedding, with bridesmaids and flower girls, and lots of kinfolks came."

June smiled at Alma. "I felt like that, too. I was scared as a field mouse, but then come the day, I did just fine. I wore one of them silky wedding dresses with lots of lace around the bodice, and everyone said I looked so pretty. I felt real pretty, too."

"I wore a satin wedding dress when I married up with Joseph Elisha," Lurina said.

"And I heard you looked right pretty." June smiled at her. "Lord, I was mad in love with Eddy." She blushed, as if she'd suddenly realized she'd spoken of too personal a matter to near-strangers.

But the other women, perhaps recalling their own wedding days, nodded and smiled as if pleased by what she said. Only May remained silent, her eyes shadowed.

Traditionally, the McCorkle women stayed to themselves. In all her years, Lurina had never driven into McCorkle Creek, never talked to any of these women, and avoided eye contact with the men. Such divisions in such a small community had always amazed Grace. Bob had said it was a matter of socioeconomics; that those who lived on Cove Road were more prosperous, and they or their kids were better educated than most of the McCorkles.

To Grace, they were all women, and as such were deeply connected to one another. "After all," she had told Bob, "we share common bonds that no man can understand: pregnancy, childbirth, and menopause." In her opinion, women were much more aware of the details of living in a way that men generally were not, and she believed women needed one another for emotional support, which their men might not be able to give them. Men got their socializing by sitting around with a bunch of guys watching a ball game or maybe working together, and many of them didn't seem to need as much overt affection as women did.

Thank God I have Hannah and Amelia in my life, Grace thought as she looked around the living room, filled with more than a dozen women. She was certain they understood what it was to support one another. Anyone could see that June and May were thick as thieves. And though Alma and Velma appeared to have little in common, they had been neighbors for years, had children about the same age and now grandchildren, and they were close.

Grace liked the energy produced in the room by this gathering of women, and she was delighted when, by the end of the evening, all the women except Bernice agreed to prod their men into helping with the painting of the church, either with labor or materials.

12

᯽

Denny Ledbetter was delighted to be asked to perform five weddings, and thrilled when Grace informed him that there would be volunteers to help get the church in top shape for the event. He wanted to sing, to dance down Cove Road, and he dashed to the parsonage to tell Pastor Johnson.

"Praise God," Johnson said. "I'm proud of you, my boy. You've done well, very well, indeed."

"It was Grace who fired up the church women, and they badgered their men. Just as I was coming over here, Ralph McCorkle brought by drop cloths, and Eddy dropped off three sturdy ladders," Denny said.

"Well, I'll be darned. Who would have thought those men would come forward like that? They aren't folks to hang about after church and chat with people on Sundays. They dash out so fast you forget they've been there. But speaking of Grace, who got her involved? Take credit for having the good sense to talk to her about this, Denny. Most other people would have listened, looked sympathetic, and not done a thing."

The members of the church council seemed pleased with everything but were considerably more reserved. Denny figured they had probably seen enthusiasm for other projects wax and wane.

"What about Christmas Eve service? How you gonna do that and marry all those couples?" Ted Lund asked.

"I discussed it with Pastor Johnson. I'd like to have a short service directly after the weddings," Denny replied. "Anyone who wants to stay can stay, and those who aren't attending the wedding but want to come to church service can do so."

"You got the strength of ten, to do five weddings and then a service," Frank said.

No one raised any objections, though they were skeptical that the church would get painted before the holidays. But once the word was out, volunteers came forward. Bob and Max, Hannah's son-in-law, Hank, and Frank and two of his sons, Tommy and Junior, were willing to help paint. Brad Herrill offered to fix the floorboards and the tilting steps. Charlie injured his back the first day carrying ladders and was prohibited from doing physical work, but he donated additional drop cloths, two extension ladders, ten gallons of paint, and a lot of moral support. If there was paint left over, they decided, they would freshen up the parsonage.

Mike's trip to Florida was canceled due to a variety of

problems. He donated paint and would photograph the work as it progressed, to create a scrapbook recording their accomplishments.

In early November the work began. "It's marvelous, the energy and the good feeling the men bring to the job," Denny told Pastor Johnson.

"You're filled with enthusiasm. They have a good model in you," the pastor said.

Nothing warmed Denny's heart more than hearing those words.

He had been warned that he might lose the man who had been like a father to him. "Not yet," he prayed silently. "Give me more time with him." The old man was so weak these days that he managed only a few hours a day in his recliner in the living room, and Denny insisted they see his doctor.

After tests, the doctor said, "You're rundown and anemic." He gave the pastor a B_{12} shot. "Bring him in next week for another shot. That should perk him up," the doctor told Denny. "That, and you seeing that he eats regular, nutritious meals. I want him up and out of that bed every day. Take him for a walk. If it's too cold out, go to the mall in Asheville or walk around the grocery store several times. Get his blood going, keep his muscles moving."

Denny talked to Grace, who supplied him with her muffins and old-fashioned chicken soup, and recipes for vegetable stew, macaroni-and-cheese casserole, and five-bean soup.

"How are you feeling today?" Denny asked Pastor Johnson after several days of the new regime.

"A bit stronger. I can sit longer at the window. The sun's good for my old bones, and doing a bit of walking's good for me. I'm grateful to you, Denny, for preparing our meals. I'd figured that was something I could handle, since you've assumed all of my other duties so quickly. I'm sorry, my boy. I've never been much of a cook, and I'm afraid I let my nutrition and my health go down the drain." The older man paused to catch his breath. "I know how busy you are, but you always make time for me, to check on me and see that I get out a bit each day."

"It's always a pleasure to be with you and to do anything to help you," Denny replied. He squeezed the old man's hand.

Pastor Johnson squeezed Denny's hand in return. "You keep up the good work, son. Charlie says you're doing great. They like your sermons. They used to like mine when I first came. The key is to keep them fresh and current, and that's not always easy. It's like a clown having to come up with a new routine every day." He smiled, and some of the humor that Denny remembered broke through like sunshine on a cloudy day.

"One time I read a joke in a magazine. It went something like this." Johnson reached for a glass of water on the end table nearby and drank, then, with a shaking hand, he set the glass back on the table. "A mother was getting her kids, six and seven years old, ready for church. Just before they left the house, she asked them, 'Why is it important that we be quiet when we're in church?' The older girl was quick to reply, 'Because people are sleeping.'"

Denny laughed. "Point well taken."

"Keep those sermons fresh, Denny. Kids tell it like it is."

The church sanctuary was small, with twenty pews on each side of the aisle, twenty-two people to a pew. Years ago, the women of the church had covered foam cushions with blue velvet fabric and placed them on the hard wooden seats. The wear and tear on the pads corresponded to the weight and girth of their traditional occupants. The seat occupied by old James McCorkle was nearly flattened, the sheen of the velvet gone under the pressure of his three hundred pounds. But there would be no time to re-cover or replace the cushions before Christmas.

Two tall stained-glass windows rose almost to the ceiling on the south-facing wall. One of the windows depicted the Nativity: the baby in the manger, a doting Mary, and Joseph welcoming the three wise men. The other showed a pregnant Mary astride a donkey with Joseph beside her, and a cherry tree dipping its branches to offer her its fruit. Dirt and smoke had dimmed their brilliant color, but soon they would be cleaned and would shine like gems.

The painting of the walls was going well. The men worked steadily, and the women took turns providing drinks and food for their menfolk. Sometimes they stayed and ate their lunches with the men, whose faces and arms were spattered with paint. They ascended and descended ladders until their legs ached, they laughed and worked continuously. The younger men, except Pastor Denny with his bad leg, would paint the highest parts of the church and would wash the stained-glass windows. May and June's mother, Ida, supplied them with her homemade vinegar water and newspapers along with copious instructions.

Ida's life had not been challenging since her husband's death two years ago. She had spent all of her married years on guard, protecting her kids and then her grandkids, keeping her "old man" from beating them when he felt like venting his frustrations about work, his health, or whatever, on the family. He could get into such a fury, but he never once raised a hand to her. He hadn't dared. Her frying pan was cast iron and heavy, and he knew she'd use it on him if he provoked her sufficiently. Now she spent her days sitting on a cushion in a pew drinking Coke after Coke and irritating the men, directing them to do this and do that. May and June were delighted to have their mother bossing someone else for a change. But Ida also regaled the painters with stories she said were the gospel truth, like the one she told them one day while they were eating their lunches.

"There was a painter named Jack over in Montgomery, Alabama, who used to cheat his clients by thinning the paint so he could make it go further. One day he got him a big church to paint on the outside, and he set to with a right good will to put up trestles and planks and buy the paint. And sure enough, he bought less paint than he charged them for and thinned the paint with water.

"Well, just about the time the job was nearly done, there was a big clap of thunder and the rain came down so hard, it washed the thin paint right off the walls of that church. The boards were so slippery, Jack fell down off the scaffold onto the lawn. He was no fool. He figured God was sending a judgment on him. He scrambled to his knees and prayed, 'Almighty God, what should I do?' A thunderous voice replied, 'Repaint! Repaint! And thin no more.'"

This brought laughter from the men.

"Go on, Miss Ida, that can't be true," Tommy said.

Ida crossed her heart with her fingers. "Swear to God, that's the story was told to me."

One morning, Denny came into the church to find a lovely crystal vase of tall pink peonies on a table near the altar. He expected one of the women to take credit for them, but they shook their heads in wonder.

"Did you bring those lovely flowers?" Denny asked Grace.

"No. My goodness, where would I get peonies this time of year?"

"Was it Amelia, do you think?"

"I don't know. Let's ask her."

But Amelia was as amazed as everyone. "I haven't seen such gorgeous flowers anywhere around here," she said.

When Hannah saw the flowers, she said, "These are either imported or grown in a hothouse, maybe down in Henderson County. Very expensive, either way."

Everyone tried to guess who had brought the flowers.

"It reminds me of the story of the dancing princesses who sneaked out every night and came home with the soles of their shoes all worn. No one ever saw them coming or going," said Molly Lund, Brenda Tate's daughter, to Hannah's daughter, Laura. The two young women worked together at Bella's Park, seeing that the re-created Covington homesteads were authentic to the last detail, and that the staff who welcomed visitors were clothed and trained in the colloquialisms and customs of that time.

"I remember that story," Laura said. "I have an idea! Why don't we camp out in the church one night and catch the flower person red-handed? It'll be fun, like we're kids again."

The young women devised a plan. On Thursday night they entered the church with their pillows, sleeping bags, flashlights, and bags of goodies, and made themselves as comfortable as possible, which was hard to do in the chilly church on hard floors or the narrow seats of a pew. As the hours passed, they shared the stories of their lives.

"I grew up on Cove Road, as you know," Molly said, "and I married right out of high school. Mom wanted me to go to college, but I refused. When I finally did go it was hard, because by then I was expecting my first son. Why do we have to be so pigheaded when we're young?"

Laura laughed. "I know exactly what you mean. If my mother said yellow, I said blue, and it went on and on like that with everything: food, clothes, the way I wore my hair, the color of my hair. I liked purple."

Molly shifted to make herself more comfortable. "Purple hair?"

"Yes. I used temporary dyes they make for costume parties."

"I didn't know they had such a thing. How did you get the color out?"

"I just gave my hair a couple of good washings," Laura said.

"What else did you fight about, you and Hannah? I'd never have had the nerve to disobey or sass my mother," Molly said. "She'd have given me a good slap if I had."

"My father did the slapping in our family. He struck my mother more than once, and she finally left him. I guess she felt guilty about yanking us out of a comfortable life, financially that is, and having to struggle so hard to make ends meet. She worked all the time to just barely pay the bills. Not a happy time in our lives."

In a timid voice, Molly asked, "Your father hit your mother?"

"She's tall, but he was bigger and taller and a mean, abusive man, apparently. Miranda remembers more about that time than I do; I was too young to understand. All I knew was that things had changed. We no longer lived by a lake; I no longer got whatever I wanted—a new pair of shoes, a doll. I was angry and behaved like a little spoiled brat."

"We don't understand what's really going on with adults when we're little, and even later on," Molly agreed. "Mom was so upset when I married Ted and didn't go to college. I thought she hated Ted, but it wasn't him so much, as that she thought once I decided not to go to college, I was limiting my options for my future. She was right, of course, and I'm glad I changed my mind. Things were better when I enrolled at UNCA. My parents helped me go to school. They invited us to live with them, helped take care of the baby when he was born, and helped us build our home. When the boys were older, Mom let them come with her to Caster Elementary, way before they were ready to actually go to school."

Laura stared into the dimly lit church. "After high school, I took a six-week course in computers. I thought I was hot stuff and could take care of myself. I ran away. I left my mother a note that said I'd gone, and she shouldn't worry about me, I'd be in touch. If I had a child who took off like that, I'd go nuts."

The church was cold. They unrolled their sleeping bags, guaranteed to keep them warm to ten degrees below zero, the tags said, and snuggled into them on the floor about halfway to the altar, or as Molly called it, the communion table. Once they were settled, Molly revived their conversation. "Where did you go when you ran away, and how did you travel?"

"I hitchhiked across the country."

"My Lord. That's so scary," Molly said. "You hear such terrible stories."

"I was darn lucky. The truckers who gave me lifts were older, decent men who tried to talk me into going home. One convinced me to call my mother and let her know I was all right. That was about three weeks after I'd left."

"I could never, ever have done that. Go off like that alone." Molly shivered. "But I envy you for having had the opportunity to live away from home and see some of the world. I went from my parents' home to my husband's, and after college I started teaching at a school a half hour from home. The most adventurous thing I've ever done was when I quit teaching and took this job at Bella's Park."

"You have deep roots. You belong, Molly. I have no roots at all. I have no place I call home."

"What do they say, the grass is always greener on the other side of the fence? Sounds like we each see something to envy in the other's life."

"I pray that Hank and I will stay in this area so that Andy can grow up feeling that he really belongs somewhere." Laura looked over at Molly. "I'm glad you took the job with Max. We'd never have known each other otherwise and become friends. Knowing you and your mom makes me feel more connected."

"We love you. I'm glad you didn't leave when your leg healed, after . . . well, you know."

Laura's brows drew together and she nodded, her face serious. "You can say it. After the storm destroyed our boat, and I lost Marvin."

"Yes. I can't even imagine how horrible that must have been."

"It was terrible, just terrible. The last thing I remember was the boom coming down and screaming at Marvin to get out of the way. How they rescued me, I don't know. When I woke up, I was in a hospital in Puerto Rico. They kept asking me who they should call. I couldn't think straight. Finally I grasped the fact that Marvin was dead, the boat at the bottom of the sea, and all my possessions with it. I guess I reverted to being a child. I wanted my mother, and I wasn't sure she'd welcome me to her new home, as sick and miserable as I was. Our relationship had always been, well, strained is a polite way of putting it, and that took time to sort itself out. It's still not perfect, but it gets better all the time, thank God.

"Amelia was the greatest help to me at that time. Once I could manage to walk, she took me with her on her photo shoots and we'd talk. We'd sit on the grass under a tree or on a smooth boulder by a stream and have a picnic she'd brought, and she'd let me rant and rave and cry my heart out. Amelia's had so much loss in her life: her child, her parents, her husband. She understood."

Molly's mother had told her how hard Laura's being there was for Hannah, and that Hannah had been at her wit's end worrying about what to do for her daughter. Now she drew the conversation back to Laura's rebellious years. "When you were young, when you were traveling around, where did you end up? Where were you going, or where did you want to go?"

Molly's interest in her life surprised Laura. She wasn't used to talking about herself or sharing those early reckless years. "Nowhere in particular. I was running away *from* my life, not toward anything. I had no destination and no goals. About a year later I hitched a ride with a trucker, a young, good-looking one, and I traveled with him for six months before I found out he had a wife and kids back in Boise, Idaho. I was furious. We were in Arizona, and that's where I got off."

Molly turned from her back onto her side so that she could see Laura better. "How did you live?"

"I waitressed."

"That seems like such hard work—on your feet all day, remembering orders and who gets what."

"It was hard, but it supported me. I hadn't learned enough in that computer class to do anything with it, and I didn't have a computer to practice on. I was also lucky. I was always able to find a female roommate to share expenses, or I got a room in some old lady's house. After my experience with the trucker, I wanted no part of men. I didn't sleep with a man again until I met Marvin."

Molly was glad for the darkness in the church to hide her blush as she said, "I've never slept with anyone but Ted." Quickly she changed the subject. "When did you go home to your family, Laura?"

"I never did, until I came here after the hurricane. I drifted out west for another year or so, then drifted east and ended up in Maine, where I met Marvin. I was buying fish." She laughed. "I didn't know one fish from the other. He was in line behind me, and when he was through explaining, I knew something about fish. He was much older than I was, and after we got together and I moved onto his boat, he insisted that I contact my mother and my sister, Miranda."

"I bet they were happy to hear from you, to know you were all right."

"They were. We stayed in touch on and off from that point. Marvin was a wonderful man, strong and wise. He taught me about sportfishing, about boats, about sailing, about running a charter boat business, and about life and love. He tried to teach me about forgiveness, but I wasn't ready. He urged me to call my mother to make up with her. I couldn't. Not then. When he died, I wanted to die. I thought I'd never stop aching for him.

"About ten months later I met Hank, and though I liked him and was attracted to him, I felt very guilty, as if loving Hank would be betraying Marvin. Hank, thank goodness, didn't give up. And slowly, as I healed and time passed, I could let myself fall in love again." Laura sat up, wrapped her arms about her knees, and leaned forward, resting her chin on her knees. "Now I have Hank and Andy, and I'm happy, Molly. And lucky. At my age, in my forties, I never expected to have a child."

Molly reached out and laid her hand on Laura's arm. "I'm glad things worked out well for you, that you're here, and that we've become friends."

They talked on for hours about their lives and their hopes and dreams for their futures.

They awakened in the morning to the sound of the church door opening and male laughter. The painters had arrived.

And a huge bouquet of red carnations now graced the table.

13

The painters started at the top of the walls, in the eaves under the peak, and worked their way down, stopping to scrub away the grime and dust that coated both of the stained-glass windows. The windows had been a gift from the estate of Griffen Anson, of all people. At the time he'd been praised posthumously for his generosity.

Now Frank Craine expressed the feelings of just about everyone when he said, "Guilt is why he gave us these windows. Anson wasn't known as a generous man. Hope that old man went to his grave feeling guilty for what he did to us."

And then, the boiler rattled and died. The temperature in the church rapidly dropped from warm to cool, from cool to chilly, from chilly to cold, to very cold. Several space heaters were brought in, but proved to be of little use.

Two heating and air-conditioning contractors were contacted and were interviewed.

"There ain't no way to fix that old junker," Ed Grimes of Grimes Heating and Cooling informed Pastor Ledbetter. "I might could get it working, but I can't guarantee it won't bust again right in the middle of Christmas service."

Lou Channing of Channing & Sons said, "Your unit's too darn old. It's a wonder it lasted this long. It's dead as dead can be. You're gonna have to replace it."

"How much?" Denny asked, dreading the reply.

And he was right to worry, for Channing said, "An electric heat pump will cost you about fifty-five hundred dollars. It'll cool you in summer, heat the place come winter."

Ed Grimes recommended a gas furnace. "Forty-five hundred's what I figure, installed," he told them. "Then there's the propane tank, but you can probably rent that. Filling it up will cost you, say, three to four hundred dollars."

"What about cooling, come summer?" asked Charlie, whom Denny had asked to attend the meetings with the heating contractors.

"You could hang ceiling fans. That would help some, or you could install separate air-conditioning units on two sides of the church," Grimes replied. "Two large ones should keep it comfortable, and it would help if you put up standing fans."

"Aren't air-conditioning wall units noisy?" Denny asked.

Grimes chewed on the end of the unlit pipe he never removed from his mouth and shrugged. "Not so much these days like they used to be. But you know how it is. You take the good with the bad."

Unhappy and uneasy with both contractors, Denny

consulted Pastor Johnson, who had little confidence in either of the men.

"People will promise you anything to get your business, and then you wait and wait and have lots of aggravation before it's done. I'm sorry I let it go so long," he said. "Things got to be more than I could handle these last couple of years. I should have asked you to come sooner."

Denny thought of how much less pain he would have experienced had the call to Covington come before Lorna Atwell arrived home from college, but it bothered him to see the old man agitated. "Don't you worry about it. You did wonderfully for many years, and these last few years you did the best you could. I'll take care of everything."

Denny prayed longer now, and more often. He watched the weather station ten times a day, saw the temperature drop and drop. The weather forecasters predicted a cold winter with snow and ice storms.

The temperatures fell even more, and the fresh roses near the pulpit wilted the day after they arrived. Denny canceled church on the last Sunday in November. It was in the thirties when he bundled up and went out to the graveyard to talk to God.

"I sure was sorry to cancel church today. We need heat. I don't care what kind, gas or electric, even an old potbellied stove, but heat. I thought about using small space heaters; about two dozen of them might do it. But Charlie, he's got an electrical business, you know, and he said we'd blow the system, maybe cause a fire, so that's out." Denny paused. *I'm a fool. What do I think is going to happen? The heavens are going to open, and God's going to appear and start talking to me?*

Bitter cold wind whipped his legs and worked its way under his fleece jacket collar and down his neck. His cheeks burned and his hands, in his gloves, felt numb. He turned and walked back to the church, to his cramped office with its single space heater.

As he approached the church, he saw a small woman walking rapidly along Cove Road. A thick fur hat and a scarf hid her mouth and chin, and he could not identify her. A red two-door car sat between the church and Maxwell's property. She slipped into it and drove away. Inside the church, the wilted roses had been replaced by a gorgeous bouquet of white lilies.

The next day the temperature rose to fifty-five and the painters added layers of clothing to resume work. Ida bundled up under a blanket in her pew.

She'd taken to singing—sometimes hymns like "Nearer My God to Thee," and sometimes songs popular back in the nineteen forties like "When the Lights Go On Again All Over the World" and another World War Two song, "Over There." "Cheers the men and helps the work along," she said. She possessed a pleasant alto voice, and Denny tried to get her to organize a choir.

"We had a choir long while back," Ida said. "Can't recall why we stopped singing."

"The roof leaked, and the piano got damaged so bad we had to dump it," Charlie said.

"I know a guy over in Weaverville who buys used pianos, fixes them up, and sells them cheap. Maybe we could

get a good deal on one or maybe a small compact organ."
This came from Tommy Craine, up on a ladder, his brush
poised in the air, paint dripping.

"You're getting the drop cloth all slippery," Ida chided
him. She ate a chicken salad sandwich May had brought
her. "Watch yourself when you come down, young fellow.
We don't need no broken bones around here." She looked
at Denny and wondered if he was sensitive about having
broken his leg falling off a ladder. It seemed a sissy thing,
falling off a ladder.

Denny made a mental note to follow up on a piano—
someday after they had a new furnace. As he walked toward
the pulpit, the thick dark curtain on the wall behind the
altar caught his eye. He'd noticed it before and assumed it
had to do with acoustics. "Should we clean that curtain?"
he asked Charlie.

"Sure, since we'll have to take it down to paint behind
it. It's been there forever. I hope it's not covering bad cracks
in the wall."

"Me, too," Denny said.

Charlie raised his voice so all could hear. "Any of you
know when this curtain was put up back here, or why?" No
one did. "If Pastor Johnson can't tell us about it, then we'll
yank it down and paint that wall, too."

When Denny asked Pastor Johnson about the curtain,
the old man shook his head. "It was there when I came.
Every time I'd go near it, the dust in it made me sneeze my
head off. I just got used to it, and after a while I never gave
it another thought."

Denny enlisted May, Grace, Velma, and Bernice to help him. With Ida directing, they yanked and pulled until the curtain gave way and plunged to the floor.

Everyone grew silent and stared openmouthed at the large framed oil painting that filled the space. It was a scene of Jesus sitting on a rock, his elbow on his knee, his chin on one hand, almost like *The Thinker* staring into a barren desert at nightfall. Before him stretched a wasteland of dark sand and black rocks, a stark and lonely landscape.

"It's a Madison Aimes painting," Denny said in a voice filled with awe.

"Who's he?" Tommy asked.

"A what painting?" Alma had just arrived at the church with hot coffee for the painters. "I never saw that before in my life. Where'd it come from?"

"The curtain was covering it up," Denny said. "Madison Aimes was a painter whose work never attained the recognition it deserved in New York, where he was born. Back in the fifties, he left New York City and went to live in a cabin in the hills of West Virginia. At first he painted local farms, but there wasn't any market among the farmers, even for a picture of their own farms. At some point, he seems to have had a religious conversion." Denny moved closer to the painting.

"One day he painted Jesus on the cross. Just Jesus, no soldiers, no women; dark boulders below and a sunset-flame sky behind. He gave the canvas to a country church in West Virginia. The minister liked it, had it framed, and hung it in the vestibule. The parishioners liked it, too. They told other people about how different it was, and over time, people who were not church members began to visit the church to see the painting."

The others gathered closer to view the painting.

"Then his cabin burned to the ground, and several paintings, too. The story is that Aimes was sleeping when the fire broke out. His dog woke him and he escaped with only his box of paintbrushes, but he felt that God had saved him. He moved on and settled in Georgia, where he vowed to donate his work to simple country churches that couldn't afford art. About thirty of his larger canvases and a few smaller ones have since found their way into museums."

"Where is he now?" Charlie asked.

"I believe he's dead, but I don't remember where I heard that. His work is extremely well regarded today."

"I'll be doggone," Charlie said. "That curtain's been there all these years, and it never dawned on any of us to take it down."

"I can see why he never got no pay for his work," Ida said. "It sure is ugly, and it don't look real, like the Bible says it was." Then her hands covered her mouth. "Pardon me, Pastor. After all, it's a picture about Jesus. But it sure is dark, like no dessert I ever seen in pictues."

"It is dark, Ida. Maybe the folks here didn't like it, and when that fellow Aimes left, they hung a curtain to cover it up," Denny said. "Pastor Johnson says the curtain was there when *he* came, but the dust made him sneeze, and he let it alone, and then forgot about it."

"If I'd been pastor, I'd have been curious to see what was behind the curtain," Bernice said.

"We all sat in church all these years, including you, and paid it no mind," June said.

"If I'd been the minister, I'd have covered it up, too," Frank said. "It's too dark. Why'd he paint it going on night I wonder? It'll scare the kids. I say we take it down, paint the wall, and brighten up the church some more."

"No, please." Denny stood in front of the painting, his arms outspread. "People will travel for hours to see this man's work. I realize that it tends to be somber, but there are scholars who study religious art, and churches that teach about Aimes's painting in religious art classes. They both consider Aimes's paintings splendid. There's a book that shows his paintings and lists where they're located."

"Well, I'll be." Frank shook his head. "Not like any painting of Jesus I've ever seen." He walked away and climbed one of the shorter ladders to resume painting.

Denny's mind raced. It would not get them their much-needed heating system now, but this painting, when recognized and authenticated by art authorities and included in the next edition of that book of Aimes's work, would bring publicity, visitors, and donations that could maintain the church for years to come. He smiled, thankful he'd come across the book about Aimes at the seminary, and grateful he'd had the opportunity to see another of Aimes's oil paintings in a small mountain church in Georgia.

14

The interior of Cove Road Church grew brighter by the day. Light bounced off the fresh white walls. Sunshine streamed through the stunning stained-glass windows, and sent rich tones of greens and blues and reds onto the drop cloths and across the cream-colored blanket that the indomitable Ida had thrown across her quilt, and under which she sat with her hat and gloves on, shivering in the chilly church.

A huge vase of pale orange roses was soon followed by slender pink lilies with lush yellow throats, followed by glorious hothouse daisies. The woman whom Denny had seen never reappeared, although he watched for her. Everyone continued to try to guess who had left the flowers. Amelia, some insisted. Others believed it was the pastor himself trying to cheer them, trying to make the work easier. Some whispered that God Himself had placed the flowers, a miracle.

Someone suggested that the flower person came to visit a relative buried in their cemetery. This idea took on credence and stirred curiosity. People began to spend more time visiting the graves of their relatives. Even in the cold, they pulled away a dried dead weed here, cleaned off a grimy headstone there. June and May visited the graves of relatives they hadn't thought of in years. They chattered with Covington folks they rarely saw and stopped to visit for a bit with Pastor Johnson, who was feeling stronger since he'd had the B_{12} shots and who was immensely cheered by all the company.

Word began to spread locally that the little church in Covington was being transformed, that it had real nice stained-glass windows, and a really strange painting of Jesus. People from a congregation over in nearby Jupiter dropped by. They arrived in a filled-to-the-brim station wagon, complained that the church was as cold inside as it was outside, and left in a hurry.

A local retirement home transported a busload of its residents, who, wrapped in coats, stood in silence or sat in pews and stared at the painting. Some considered it blasphemous. Some were deeply moved by it. Some were sure that Jesus would not like it.

"Probably painted by a heathen," a woman muttered.

Others praised the work.

Ida appointed herself the guide and ushered visitors around the little church as the painting of the walls continued. Always good at storytelling, she made up a tale about the history of the church. "It was founded by two families who used to live 'round these parts," she told the visitors.

"One of the families had a son, the other a daughter, and they fell in love. Both families were right set against their marrying. Old family feud over land and cattle; you know how that can be."

People from Madison County knew about feuds, shootings, and families not speaking for generations. Although folks today laughed and joked about it, it wasn't known as bloody Madison County for nothing.

"So." Ida sighed and proceeded. "The young'uns run off, and Lordy mercy if they don't get killed in an awful train wreck. Their families felt so bad, they joined up and gave the money to build this here church." She nodded sagely. "This little ole church was built on sorrow."

"What are you telling those people?" Charlie asked her one day.

"Some of those folks come a far piece to see our church. Might as well give 'em a story to take home to tell their kin." Ida, at eighty-one, considered Charlie, who had just turned seventy, too young to question her.

Charlie shook his head and walked away. He knew Ida wouldn't listen to anything he said anyhow, and the pastor seemed to have no objection. He let it drop.

Denny found the first of the money half hidden under the crystal vase. It was a fifty-dollar bill. The next anonymous contribution was a twenty, the next two bills were fives, and then a hundred-dollar bill. Denny placed a small mahogany box he bought at Roses in Weaverville next to the flowers with a note: "Thank you and may the Lord bless you!" He showed the cash to Pastor Johnson.

"The Lord does indeed move in mysterious ways," the pastor said. Then he asked, "What did you decide about the Christmas Eve service?"

"I'm going to announce it for five P.M., just after the weddings."

"You might have a small turnout, unless all those folks at the weddings stay on."

"I don't think they will stay; there are parties afterward. We're invited both to Bernice's, who's having a joint reception with May and June, and to Alma and Velma's shindig at Velma's home. I told them we'd have to come late. It'll work out."

Charlie had had word from his attorney. Any property, home, land, or car that was already in both names was fine and would pass without taxes to the other, should one of them die. But if any of it was still in a husband's or wife's name alone, that would not pass directly, unless there was a will with those instructions.

"It's all so complicated," Bernice complained.

"What about our children?" Ralph asked.

"Where the kids are concerned, the same again if we were to get us killed in a car crash tomorrow, God forbid. If any of us is gonna put off marrying, it would be best to get a signed affidavit down at the courthouse, with witnesses, to say the kids belong to us and were born on such and such a date and so on."

"I think we're doing the right thing getting married right quick, and I just pray we all stay healthy and alive the next couple of weeks," Frank said.

"Lordy mercy," Bernice said. "You got me scared to go in the car to the grocery store now."

"Just be careful," Charlie said. "I'm sure it'll be just fine. It's just a few weeks now until Christmas Eve."

Later, June asked Eddy, "I know we own this house in both our names, but who owns all that land back up the hill, honey?"

"Ma owned it from Pa, and she willed it to me when she died."

"What should we do, go get it changed to you and me?"

"If you want to, but it's gonna cost us money."

"We gotta do it even after we marry, for the taxes, right?" June asked.

Eddy looked puzzled for a moment. "Well, I reckon you're right. We might as well just go on ahead and get it done."

When June broached the matter of property and ownership to May, May refused to talk about it.

Alma hadn't gotten on well with her in-laws, yet when they died, everything went to her and Frank together. "They done it that way," Alma had said to Frank at the time, "so's I'd feel guilty all my born days."

"Guilty for what?"

"For feeling the way I did about them. Not being as patient or good as I could be with 'em," Alma replied.

Frank put his arm around her shoulder. "Alma, you were

a saint. Ma was no easy person to live with. I think you did right fine by her. You don't have anything to feel bad about."

Velma and Charlie already owned everything jointly, even his business, which was a corporation and of which she was a board member.

As they began to make these changes, the couples began to relax and feel better about their situations. The women, especially, could more easily turn their minds to their weddings, which were fast approaching.

As she began to prepare for her wedding, Alma still had many questions. "Is it really going to work, all our weddings on the same day? What if it's freezing in the church? We can't ask people to sit and shiver through five weddings. And what if our guests stay on for the service afterward? It was foolish of us to have our weddings on Christmas Eve. We ought to have done them sooner."

"Oh, Alma, stop fussing. Everything's going to be just fine," Velma said. They were at the mall in Asheville in a women's clothing store, trying on outfits appropriate for a wedding. "I think we ought to buy pantsuits instead of dresses," Velma continued. "That way if it's cold in church, we can keep warm by wearing long johns under our clothes."

"Buy a pantsuit? What am I gonna do with it afterward? I'm too old to be wearing pants."

"And too stingy," Velma retorted.

"I don't care what you say. I don't waste money, especially on clothes I'm only going to wear one time," Alma replied.

Velma pointed at the pale yellow chiffon cocktail dress Alma had tried on from the sales rack. "But you'll wear this again? For what occasion, may I ask? Besides, if you wear this dress you'll freeze before you walk down the aisle."

Alma hugged the dress to her and spun around. "I don't much care. I love this dress, and the price is right. It makes me feel pretty. Besides, I won't freeze in that short a time."

"You're not making sense. You think people can't sit in the church in the cold, but you won't freeze while wearing a flimsy summer dress? Well, you just do whatever you want, Alma. I'm buying me a nice suit that I can wear something warm under."

But Alma would not be dissuaded. She handed the dress to the saleswoman along with her credit card.

"What do you think May and June are gonna wear?" she asked Velma, who laughed.

"Something their mama Ida sews up for them, probably."

What to wear was indeed a dilemma for the McCorkle twins. May said, "I told Billy I had to have money for a new dress."

"What'd he say?"

"He ain't said nothing. Just looked at me as if I'd gone clear outta my mind."

"Eddy says he don't want to do this anyhow, so if I ain't got nothing to wear it's just as well, and we can forget about it." June narrowed her eyes. "Of course, he's got a nice suit from when he was a pallbearer last year."

"You know how Mama is. She won't let them forget about it—not if she's got to cut up quilts and sew dresses for us."

"May, you go on so! Mama cut up a quilt? She'd as soon swim naked in a cold river."

"Well, what are you planning to wear, June?"

"I got some money I been putting away to buy me a sewing machine. I figure instead of pestering Eddy, I'll use it for a dress. Then later, I'll get after him to buy me the sewing machine. Fact is, May, I have almost enough for two dresses from Target or Kmart. We could each get us one."

May's eyes lit up at the prospect of a new dress. She didn't want to marry Billy again, but since she had to because of their kids, she might as well wear something pretty. "That would be nicer than showing up in some old thing from the back of my closet. How much more money do we need for two dresses? I'll take it from Billy's pockets a dollar at a time till we get what we need."

The twins laughed. It felt good to laugh; May hadn't laughed in a very long time.

Mike recognized the Aimes and was thrilled when he saw it. He recommended, and Bob offered to foot the bill for, an artist in Asheville to clean and restore the painting. Denny entrusted the Aimes to Mike's care.

Then Mike and Amelia set about planning the flowers for the wedding, which Charlie offered to pay for. They decided on white mums for their price and availability in December, with a pop of red Christmas ribbons, to fill the space in front of the pulpit and altar. More mums, tied with clusters of red ribbons and bows, would be hung on the center ends of the pews. Mums would decorate the tables in the vestibule of the church, and if the weather were sunny and not too cold, they would wrap pots in shiny red paper and set them on the entry steps to brighten the walk into the church. Wreaths splendid with poinsettias would decorate the entrance doors of the church and the vestibule doors.

Amelia left a note for their mysterious flower benefactor.

Dear flower person,
There will be five weddings here on December 24, beginning at two in the afternoon. We will be using white mums to decorate, tied about with red ribbons. We'd appreciate your coordinating your flowers with ours for this very special occasion.

Sincerely, an admirer,
Amelia Declose

P.S. You are more than welcome to attend the weddings. I would so enjoy meeting you.

When Denny informed her that her note had vanished and that none of the painters or women had taken it, Amelia was delighted.

15

⚜

One afternoon, Denny Ledbetter called a meeting of the church council to decide about the heat, and about the Aimes painting. Pastor Johnson started outside with Denny to attend the meeting, but the cold stung his face and hands and penetrated his several layers of clothing.

"I can't even breathe out there, it's so cold. I'd best stay indoors. Express my apologies and explain why I couldn't make it to the meeting, will you, my boy?"

"Of course. You're wise to stay inside. Don't you worry; I'll bring back a full report."

The old man looked less wan and pale since receiving several B_{12} shots, but he was still a ways from being his old self. It frightened Denny, how long it was taking. He helped Pastor Johnson back into the parsonage and settled him into his armchair by the fire.

"I tell you, my boy, aging is a difficult and discouraging process. In my mind I feel young, interested, and eager to go and do, but my body has a mind of its own—a mind that rules."

"Would you consider taking a few weeks and visiting your sister in Florida? She keeps calling and inviting you. You'll be stuck in the house all winter here. If you go, you'll return home perked up and feeling great after a couple of weeks in the sunshine. Think about it, will you?"

"You trying to get the house to yourself, son?" Pastor Johnson teased Denny. "I'd rather spend this winter—and Lord knows, it might be my last—here with you."

Denny felt the hair rise on his arms.

At the meeting Denny had called, six sober men sat around a table set up in Denny's office, where a space heater kept the temperature livable, and stared at the estimates for heating units and at Denny's proposal regarding the Aimes painting.

He told them that the painting was being cleaned and refurbished. Mike had taken it to the restoration artist who worked for the Biltmore House, and Bob was paying the bill. The painting should be back and rehung by Tuesday of next week. He urged them to waste no time in inviting an art historian and appraiser to view the Aimes. The invitation should come from the council rather than from himself, but he could get the names of some reputable people to look at it.

They agreed, set that proposal aside, and looked serious as they studied the estimates for replacing the furnace.

"Channing's a good man. He did the heat pump for our farmhouse, two units in fact—one for upstairs, one for down—when we rebuilt after the fire," Frank said.

Charlie nodded. "Channing did mine, too. He does good work and he's proposed an electric unit this time."

"Sometimes he's off on his timing, like when the men are supposed to come at a certain time or on a particular day and they don't show," Frank said. "But when they do come, they do good work."

"I have no preference," Denny said. "I don't know either one of them. But where's the money coming from? Miss Pratt says there's not one red cent."

Heads shook. Frank crossed his arms. "She's right. There's no money. It can't be done right now. I'm sorry."

"There must be some way," Denny said. "We can't just close the church."

"Now, Pastor," Ted Lund said. "We've had times when the old furnace went out on us, and we just rounded up a couple of space heaters and set them up around the church."

"I've told you before, too many space heaters will blow the fuses. They could cause a fire." Charlie repeated the warning.

"Yes, I know," Ted replied. "But say the church is about fifty-five degrees, and we plug in some heaters a couple of hours before the service starts. They'll take the chill off and bring the temperature to maybe sixty or sixty-five degrees. That's tolerable if you bundle up real good. The rest of the time, the place is empty."

"Five thousand dollars seems like a lot of money for a new heat pump, especially when the place only gets used one day a week for an hour or so," Alvin Edmunds said.

Charlie had briefed Denny prior to the meeting. Miserly Alvin was married to Eddy McCorkle's fourth cousin. Denny had met Alvin's type before: a person guaranteed to contribute nothing positive, who could be depended upon to be a naysayer.

"If you'll look at the last sheet, it's another proposal. You know we have a rare Aimes painting that belongs to our church. After we have it authenticated and added to the book that lists the churches with his work, people would come to see it, and they would make donations that would help us a lot. The exterior of the church needs painting. The roof is going to need fixing in a year or so, and there are other floorboards that are loose. We could have a serious accident. Then there are the pews, which need restaining, and places where the stain on the floor is completely worn through. If we put the word out about the painting to other church groups in the area, it could take care of all the church maintenance for years to come."

"How come if we got so many problems, Pastor Johnson never said nothing about them?" Alvin asked.

A deep silence fell on the room. No one wanted to say what was on their minds: that the pastor had been ill for a longer time than any of them realized, or that he had chosen not to make waves, to do nothing that would draw attention to himself and his growing disability.

Ralph McCorkle spoke up. "Pastor, are you saying our church should be like a freak show, with all kinds of people coming and going just to see that grim-looking picture?"

"Goodness no, Mr. McCorkle. The visitors would be

mainly churchgoers and most respectful. I took a group of parishioners to a church over in north Georgia one time to see a work by Aimes. We stood or sat quietly and appreciated the work. People left gifts, contributions for the painting's and the church's upkeep."

"Sounds dumb to me," Alvin Edmunds said.

Charlie studied Denny's proposal. "Pastor Johnson seen this?" He looked intently at Denny.

"He has. I took him into Asheville yesterday to see the painting."

"And all these years he never looked behind that drape?" Alvin asked. "Mighty peculiar, I'd say." Everyone ignored Alvin's comment.

"Pastor Johnson thinks that acknowledging it's an Aimes and having people come to see it is a grand idea," Denny said.

"So you feel that heating the church, replacing the old machine, is necessary if we're gonna get people to visit the church to see that painting. And you say that folks who visit churches with these paintings make contributions?" Charlie asked.

"I do, sir, and yes, from what other ministers have told me, visitors are most generous."

"Well, I'll be darned. Maybe there's something to this ugly old picture," Ralph said.

"I assure you, there is." Denny removed an envelope from his jacket pocket. "Look at this. In just the last few weeks, we've been given six hundred and twenty dollars."

"Who from?" Frank asked.

Alvin Edmunds leaned forward, interested now.

"We don't know. The first money was left under the vase of fresh flowers with one end of a bill sticking out. Then we got more. I placed a small box there, and since then, there's money in that box nearly every day. Sometimes a ten, sometimes a fifty, twice a hundred-dollar bill."

Charlie let out a whistle. "Well, I'll be damned."

"You've never seen anyone do it?" Hank was new to the board.

Denny could tell from the way he spoke that he was not from this area. Hank was a landscape architect chosen by George Maxwell to help design Bella's Park, and he was married to Hannah's daughter, Laura, who also worked for the park.

"No. I have not."

"Well, I'll be damned," Charlie said again, then looked at Denny. "Pardon my language, Pastor."

"Swearing in the Lord's house, Charlie?" Frank grinned. He had done his share of swearing at past council meetings.

"Look, fellows," Charlie said. "Time's running out. We got five weddings coming up. The church is looking better than it has in years, and none of it has cost the church a cent. There are six of us here. I say we match this six hundred and fifty dollars out of our pockets by each putting in a hundred dollars."

"We could ask Max to contribute. And I'm sure Bob Richardson would, too," Hank said.

"That's a good idea, Hank. You handle that. Then we'll go to the bank and borrow the rest and get the darn heater fixed," Charlie said. He rubbed his palms together in a "that's settled, then" manner.

"We're putting this to a vote," Frank reminded him.

Charlie sighed. Lord, he hated not being able to just go ahead, make a decision, and get the thing done. "All in favor?"

Frank's hand went up, followed by Ted's, Charlie's, Hank's, and Ralph's, which surprised Denny. Alvin looked away.

"It's okay, Alvin," Charlie said. "We all got to vote our own conscience."

"I ain't puttin' up no money."

"If that's how you feel, it's okay."

Alvin unsteadily rose to his feet, staggered, and nearly fell, and Denny realized that the man was drunk. He offered up a silent prayer for him and wondered how they could replace him on the council.

"You go ahead, Pastor, and call Channing," Charlie said. "Time's short. We'll be lucky if he can order the system and have it installed in time for Christmas Eve. Tell him to get in touch with me if he's got a problem."

16

On December 8, Channing's men thumped, banged, and cursed as they broke apart the rusty old furnace and hauled it up the basement steps, dragged it to their van, and carted it away.

Channing appeared in the doorway of Denny's office, a clipboard in his hand. "We're done for now."

"You have the new unit?" Denny asked.

"Not yet. The church waited mighty late to order one."

"I thought you were going to put a rush on the order," Denny said.

"I have, but I can't guarantee you getting it installed by Christmas Eve, what with everybody so busy around the holidays."

Denny heard the negativity in the man's voice. Pastor Johnson was right: trouble was brewing. "I know it's late, and I appreciate what you're saying," he replied. "We didn't have the funds. I beg you to do all you can to get it here. Where is it coming from?"

Channing flipped pages on his pad. "From Charlotte."

"That's so close. Can't you send a truck down there to pick it up? We'd pay the extra."

"Ain't so much the money, Pastor. It's the time. Everyone's got an emergency this time of year. I'll do my best."

By December 17, Denny had still not heard from Channing. An answering machine with a pleasant female voice took his calls, but his messages were not returned. Denny started biting his nails, an old habit abandoned years ago. Bundling up against the chill of the day, he headed for the parsonage, speaking all the while to God.

"I don't have to tell you what's been going on, Lord. You know it all. I'm asking you to help us by speeding up the heat pump and getting it installed before Christmas Eve. I've been so busy, so worried, I haven't even prepared for the weddings. Five, one after the other—what do you think of that?"

As he passed the cemetery, a woman's voice called, "Pastor." The voice was very soft, with an accent, maybe French.

Denny turned. A woman, neither young nor old, stood before a tombstone a dozen graves away. She was slender, and her sharp cheekbones drew attention to her eyes, which were round and large and gray as a winter sky heavy with snow. "Marguerite Le Blanc." Her tiny hand disappeared in Denny's firm handshake. *"S'il vous plaît,* may we speak inside?"

He escorted her across the uneven ground of the cemetery. His office, at least, was warmed from the space heater. Denny pulled out the extra desk chair for her. She seemed high-strung, nervous, he thought.

"You saw me once before. I wanted not to be noticed. I want to help the church." Without fanfare, she opened her purse and handed Denny a check.

His eyes grew wide. "Five thousand dollars?"

"I know you need heat for the church." She removed her gloves, folded them neatly, and rested them in her lap.

"Thank you! Thank you! But why, Mrs. Le Blanc?"

Marguerite settled back into the chair and crossed her legs. Her ankles were small and trim, like the ankles Denny imagined a dancer might have. "My grandparents are buried in your *cimetière.*"

"Really? What are their names?"

"Louise Devereau Covington and George Covington. They met in France after the big war, fell in love, and married. My grandfather brought her to Covington, to his *famille.*" Marguerite shook her head. She was *triste,* unhappy, like, how you say, a fish out of the water. She died a year later giving birth to *ma mère.*

"My grandfather loved her very much and could not live without her, they said. He drove into a bridge. An accident? *Mais, non.* The Covington family were crazy with grief. They let her parents take the baby, my mother, Marie, back with them to France. It is very sad, no?"

"Very sad, indeed. And you have been visiting their graves and gracing us with such beautiful flowers?" The miracle check tingled between Denny's fingers. His heart raced. "You are most generous. I hardly know what to say."

"There is nothing to say. Just accept, and use it well."

"How did you manage to place the flowers? We've all wondered. No one ever saw you."

"Ah, well. In the beginning no one came very much to the church, and I could slip in and out unnoticed. When people began to paint the walls, I must come very early then. Once I hid behind the curtain. I got out at noon when the painters went for lunch. I saw the Aimes. I was an artist in my younger days. I knew Aimes. He died, you know, about five years ago in Paris. He was very old, nearly a hundred years old. I used to visit with him, take him pastries. He loved pastries. I was behind the curtain; I heard about the heat and felt the cold."

She paused, then continued in her charmingly accented voice. "A church must warm a person in their hearts, but also their bodies. I hope you will accept this small donation from me, from my daughters, and my husband. All I ask is that you arrange to have someone tend my grandparents' graves."

"Certainly. Let's walk outside, and you can show me exactly where their graves are." Denny stood, bumped into his desk, and felt like a country bumpkin.

"*Oui.*" She rose and began to slip an arm into her coat.

Denny rounded the desk and assisted her. Her lovely oval face disappeared under a mound of fur when she settled her hat firmly on her head and pulled it down to cover her ears. He tried to guess her age. She spoke of daughters, obviously old enough to have an opinion about their mother handing over a check for five thousand dollars. She was forty, maybe forty-five?

They moved slowly among the graves, careful of up-turned stones and depressions in the grass, until she stopped before two graves that were easy to miss, since their stones were smaller and shorter than those around them. Moss grew in the deeply chiseled letters and lichen sprawled across the old marble, worn rough with time. The names chiseled on the stones were barely decipherable, but Denny could clearly distinguish the capital *c*s in Covington, the *l* in Louise, and the *d* in Devereau.

"In the beginning, the flowers I bring for them," Marguerite said. "But in the cold they die and my grandparents cannot see them, of course, so I leave them inside the church for all to enjoy. I wanted time here to visit the area, to feel where they lived, how they lived. I visited Bella's gardens too and the homestead where the ancestors lived."

Denny rubbed his chin. "Mrs. Le Blanc, I'm here to assist Pastor Johnson, who's been the pastor of this church for many years. He's quite elderly and hasn't been well. Can you spare a few minutes to come with me to the parsonage? It's that little clapboard cottage over there. I know he would take great pleasure in meeting you. He's a great admirer of your lovely flowers and has decided they are the gifts of an angel."

"Of course. I would be happy to meet your Pastor Johnson."

Taking her elbow, Denny guided her along the uneven ground and onto the concrete pathway that led to the parsonage. He opened the front door and called, "Pastor Johnson, I've brought a guest. Your angel, the lady who's given us the lovely flowers, is here and would like to meet you."

A tremulous voice replied, "What a lovely gift on this cold day. Please come in, and welcome."

The room they entered was low ceilinged and cozy. Sunlight streamed through tall windows and cast beams of light across the handwoven rag rugs that covered large portions of the old oak floors, scuffed and worn pale in places. Hand-crocheted doilies covered the back and arms of the well-worn sofa, and a cheery fire blazed behind faux logs in the gas fireplace that had been installed last year when Pastor Johnson could no longer manage a wood fire.

"Please, sit down," Pastor Johnson said. "Denny, my boy, would you fix us some tea and bring some of Grace's cookies? And use the good china, will you?"

From the large overstuffed armchair, Marguerite studied the old man sitting across from her. From the manner in which the quilt was draped across his legs, she assumed that he was an invalid and perhaps unable to stand on his own. Although his face was heavily lined and his white hair sparse, his eyes were alert, interested, and cheerful, and belied his age.

"My dear," he said. "Your beautiful flowers have given all of us great pleasure. To what do we owe such generosity?"

He listened attentively as Marguerite explained about her grandparents, and all the while the clink of silver, of china cups placed on their saucers, and the sound of a kettle whistling on the stove issued from the kitchen. Once Denny's head appeared around the door. "Nearly ready," he said.

"Take your time, son," Pastor Johnson said. "I'm enjoying having this delightful lady all to myself."

"Pastor Denny is your son?" Marguerite sounded confused.

"No. Denny is like my son," Pastor Johnson said. "Like a very good and loving son to me."

"*Oui,* I understand. Sometimes the saying that blood is thicker than water is not true, yes?"

The old man nodded.

Denny entered and set the tray on the coffee table, then poured tea from a delicate floral china teapot into matching cups.

"How very lovely your china is. It is French, Limoges."

"Indeed it is. It was my mother's," Pastor Johnson said.

"A fine old pattern. It is hard to find these days and very valuable," she said.

"I never had it appraised, but I assumed as much. I have always preferred tea in a beautiful cup," the pastor said. "I hate it when I am served tea in a thick mug."

"I very much agree," she replied.

"My wife and I inherited this set, when my mother passed."

Denny was stunned. Pastor Johnson had been married? Why didn't he know this?

Marguerite added milk and sugar to her tea, and stirred. "And your wife?"

A shadow crossed the old man's face, and then he smiled at Marguerite. "She was a good woman. Very intelligent. Very kind. Unfortunately we were married only a short time, two very lovely years, and she was gone." He set his cup down. "She died in childbirth. Our son, Emile, was premature and he lived only ten days before joining her in God's heaven. A lung condition. In those days, so many women and babies died from things that today are so easily cured."

"I am so sorry. I did not mean to bring up such a sad matter."

"It's all right. I rarely speak of her." He looked at Denny. "Oh, my poor boy. You're stunned by this revelation. Forgive me, I should have told you long ago. Sometimes I forget. It's all so long ago, and sometimes I simply prefer not to remember. I'm sorry. I should have told you."

His not telling Denny hurt, reminding him that in reality he was not the pastor's son. For no matter how often the old man might call him that, a real son would know about such a devastating matter.

Marguerite looked from one man to the other. "You are related, though, yes?"

"I grew up in a orphanage," Denny told her. There was a time when just thinking that someone had not wanted him, had given him away, pained and shamed him, and he had avoided any discussion about the orphanage. But over time, he had come to terms with the issue of abandonment and had forgiven the unknown girl or woman who was his biological mother. Surely her situation had not been a happy one, and pointless though it was, he still sometimes wondered where she was and if she ever thought about him.

"And I spent my vacations ministering at the summer camp that was held on the orphanage grounds. That's where we met. Denny was only seven at the time," Pastor Johnson was saying.

"And desperately in need of a father's attention and affection," Denny said. He knew the hurt of not being confided in would pass, as so many hurts passed.

"Yes, he was the saddest, sweetest little seven-year-old boy I ever saw. He was so small. His hair was like the color of straw then. If I could have taken him home, I would have, but in those days they didn't allow single men to adopt a child."

He would have adopted me! Legally, he would be my father. How very good to know that.

Johnson looked pointedly at Denny. "Denny *is* a son to me—the son I lost, replaced by God, and here now to soothe my soul."

"And you never wanted to remarry?" Denny asked.

"Never, my boy. I couldn't bear to go through a loss of such magnitude ever again."

Marguerite raised a hand apologetically. *"Je vous prie de m'excuser.* I have asked too many questions. I am so sorry."

"It was a long time ago. Then I came here, and my congregation became my family. I have been here a very long time."

"Forty years," Denny said. "A very long time." His gaze settled on the old man, the love unmistakable in his eyes.

"If I had been his actual son, Pastor Johnson could not have treated me more lovingly or done more for me. He blessed me with his wise counsel, never forgot my birthdays or Christmas, and he visited whenever he could. This man"– he patted Johnson's shoulder gently–"gave me my first pair of high boots. And later, when I exhibited a modicum of skill with a guitar, he bought me one." He swallowed hard and looked into Marguerite's eyes. "I would never have been able to go to college or to the seminary without his generosity."

"So as a good son, you have come to be with him now?"

"Yes."

"Denny left a fine congregation for my sake. They hated to see him go. But if he had not answered my request to come here, they would have had to put me away in some old folks' home by now."

"You are blessed to have each other," Marguerite said. Her eyes traveled to the Swiss clock on the far wall. A brown bird, its head permanently tilted to the right, announced the time to be three P.M. She rose. "I am sorry, but I must go. I must take my rental car back to the airport and catch a plane. I meet my husband and family in New York this evening. Today, I came here especially to talk to Pastor Denny and to give him a check."

Pastor Johnson's eyebrows rose, unasked questions in his eyes.

She smiled at him, then bent and kissed his cheek. "Pastor Denny will tell you later."

Denny helped her into her coat; then she turned once

more to the older man. "Amelia wrote a sweet note inviting me to your weddings. I am returning soon to Paris with my family and cannot come to the weddings. I am sorry; I would have enjoyed that very much. I have arranged with a *fleuriste* in Mars Hill to deliver flowers to the church every Saturday for the next year in memory of my grandparents." She turned to Denny. "And you must promise me that when they arrive, you will bring to Pastor Johnson the best flower in the vase so that he will remember me."

Pastor Johnson made a valiant effort to rise, and stood on shaky legs. "Madame, I will remember you always."

Marguerite wrapped her scarf snugly about her neck. Perhaps it was the scarf, perhaps it was the trim, bright quality of the woman, but at that moment she reminded Denny of Amelia.

"I'm sorry the others can't meet you, Amelia especially," Denny said. "She lived in France for many years."

"She is my favorite of the people who come to the church. Will you tell her that for me?"

"Yes. Let me walk you to your car."

He looked for the red car and saw only a blue station wagon.

Marguerite smiled at him. "I surprise you, yes? I change cars, so I am not, how you say, conspicuous when I come and go." She unlocked the car door. "You are a good man, Pastor Denny. It is a pleasure to meet you and your Pastor Johnson. Take care of him. He loves you very much. And I know you will see that my grandparents' graves are taken care of."

"I will indeed take care of the pastor, and see that the graves are well tended, Mrs. Le Blanc."

"Marguerite, please."

"Marguerite. It was a great pleasure to meet you, and again, thank you on behalf of myself and the entire congregation for your most generous gift."

"It will not be the last, my friend." She slid into the car and drove away. When he could no longer see the taillights of the car, he wondered if he had dreamed her, until he returned to his office, held the check to the light, and once more marveled at the generosity of the woman.

Later that day, Denny stepped out onto Cove Road and stared up at the weathered paint of the church. In these few months it had evolved from being just a church to being "his" church, and Marguerite Le Blanc's gift would make it possible to paint the exterior when the weather warmed up, perhaps in time for Easter.

17

⚜

The night was cold. All afternoon, gray clouds rolled thick and portentous across the sky, and the scent of snow impregnated the air. Inside the ladies' living room, a roaring fire spread warmth. Grace served hot spiced apple cider and peach pie as the final gathering of the five brides-to-be began.

"It appears," Velma said, "that our new minister is trying his very best. Charlie tells me that he's on the phone every day with Channing, and so is Charlie, but you know how it is with these people. First they gotta have your money to order the goods, and then you sit and wait, and they have the advantage over you because they've got your money in their pockets. I wouldn't count on heat in that church for Christmas or our weddings. I think we have to plan for all possibilities."

"We'll freeze," Alma said. "Why don't we postpone the weddings? Why do we have to be married on Christmas Eve anyhow?" She visualized herself in the yellow dress, in springtime, among the daisies.

"I told you to buy a pantsuit," Velma said, and Alma looked aggrieved.

"I can still get one." Alma picked at a loose piece of wool on the front of her red cardigan sweater.

Bernice folded her hands across her ample middle and smirked. "What are you, sissies? Can't tolerate a little cold for the short time it takes to get married?"

A smug look passed between June and May. Ida had convinced them that the heat would not be fixed in time for Christmas, and they had bought pantsuits at Target, and they had long johns just in case.

Grace began, "Well, if you decide to cancel—"

"I ain't canceling nothing," Bernice said. "We got family coming up from Georgia and South Carolina. We got a reception with food and music planned for afterward."

"Then let's go over the procedures for the weddings," Grace said. "We drew lots and it came out that June is first, followed by Alma, then Bernice, May, and Velma, you'll be last."

"Fine with me. Last is as good as first."

"Seems the Bible says something like that." May surprised herself with her comment, and was relieved when no one picked up on it.

"Pastor's rented a piano," Hannah said. "Mrs. Todman from over in Jupiter is going to play the wedding march and the recessional. No one indicated a preference for any other music, so it'll be that simple. May, June, Bernice, and Alma all want a traditional ceremony. Velma and Charlie have written their own vows."

Velma looked pleased.

Bernice's mind wandered. She found Alma and Velma boring. Pulling back the curtains of time, Bernice saw herself as the young woman she had been, full chested but with a slim waist and legs the boys whistled at when she went with her friends to the swimming hole at the old quarry. Her mother had been of Spanish descent, her father an Appalachian man and a McCorkle, in whose veins streamed love of his land.

Ralph's people had the tract of land that butted up to her father's family's land. They had grown up together, and because they bore the same last name, they sat near each other in every class from first grade to high school graduation. She hadn't liked him much. He teased her, and when he sat behind her, he would tug on her long black hair, sometimes knotting it when the teacher's back was turned.

Bernice had graduated high school with honors in math, gone to AB Tech, and received her certificate in bookkeeping. She'd been working at a construction company when she met up with Ralph a few years later. He walked in that door with a swagger, his jeans low on his hips, and looked at her blankly for a moment until recognition dawned. "Well, I'll be darned. Bernice, is that you?"

"Where've you been all these years, Ralph?"

"Come have lunch with me and I'll tell you."

She did. And to dinner, and to baseball games, and to

hear Johnny Cash when he came to sing down in Green-ville, South Carolina. Six months later, she married him. Bernice thought she was getting a decisive man, but it turned out that Ralph's swagger was all cover-up. He asked her opinion on everything—who to vote for come election time, and what he should do on Sunday after church: watch a ball game, go fishing, take one of their kids to a movie in Asheville?

"You know about keeping books," he said a few weeks after they were married, and handed her his paycheck. "You keep the money."

Keeping money was what she did at work, not some-thing she wanted to do at home. But she found out soon enough that Ralph wasn't good with money. When he'd get his hands on it, seemed like the green dollar bills caught on fire and burned a hole in his pocket. He bought toys for the kids and man-sized toys, like trucks and farm machinery that they didn't need, for himself. When he brought home the Harley, they had a huge fight, and he'd handed her his credit card.

He was hardworking, Ralph was, and a big kid, too, the way he played with their children, chasing them around the sofa in the sitting room, tickling them till they begged for mercy. For all his good looks and those bedroom eyes, though, he wasn't much in bed. She got used to that, too. She went on working, and still did, for the same construc-tion company. They'd moved their office to Canton, so the drive was a far piece now, especially in winter, what with the snow and icy roads every now and then.

Bernice had gained weight. Who was there to be attractive and sexy for? Once the kids were gone, she and Ralph slept in separate bedrooms. It was easier than lying next to him and sometimes feeling sexy and his turning away from her, saying he was just too tired. She'd read in one of those magazines, maybe it was *Cosmopolitan*, that sometimes food was a substitute for sex. It sure was for her.

Amelia's voice drew her back to the present, to the other women and the weddings. "Perhaps you haven't heard, but a French woman, the person who left the beautiful flowers in the church, came to see Pastor Denny," Amelia was saying. "Seems she's got grandparents buried in the cemetery. She gave the pastor a big donation, and she's paid for flowers to be sent to the church every Saturday for a year in honor of her grandparents."

"Well, bless her heart, ain't that something," May said.

"Who's her kin?" Bernice asked. "I don't recall a French family ever living here. I'd remember; they got names that are hard to pronounce. You can nearly choke saying them."

"The story's such a sad, romantic one, like Romeo and Juliet." With dramatic flourishes of her hands, her eyes gleaming, Amelia related the story of the sad young bride, her death in childbirth, the new husband's overwhelming grief and death, and how the Covington family let the French family take the baby back to France.

There were tears in Alma's eyes. "I can't believe the Covingtons sent that baby girl away."

"Probably 'cause it was a girl. Bet they'd have kept a boy carrying their name," June said.

"Just like them people. A McCorkle would never have done that," Bernice said.

"Well, ain't that a shame," May said. "Wonder if Harold Tate knew about that, and if he was related to the ones that sent that baby back to France? Harold was the last of the Covingtons around these parts."

Grace said, "His kin are still Covingtons. Molly and Ted Lund's boys have Covington blood."

"I wonder if Brenda Tate knew about all this," June said.

"We could ask her next time we meet up with her," May said, knowing that she would never casually meet up with Brenda Tate. And if by chance she did, say in the market, they might nod but not stop to chat.

June smiled at her sister, thinking that if not for this wedding business, they would not know the Cove Road women or the Yankee women. She realized that she liked them all, and that they were not so different in their concerns from her or May.

Hannah said, "Ladies, we don't want to keep you too late." She went to the window and peered up at the sky, dark and somber over the mountains beyond Maxwell's dairy farm. "It looks like it's going to snow tonight. Let's quickly go over the procedures for the wedding, then I think we ought to call it quits."

She consulted her clipboard, on which the stack of papers multiplied by the day. "After June and Eddy take their vows, they'll walk back up the aisle and take seats in the last row, which I've reserved for the wedding parties. Alma will be waiting in the vestibule. I'll be there the whole time, of course, and Amelia and Grace, too. The wedding march will start again. I will give you the sign, Alma, and you'll start down the aisle. Who's escorting you?"

"Tommy's gonna do it."

"Your son, that's nice," Hannah said. "You got a bridesmaid or flower girl?"

"My grandbabies all want to walk in front of us."

"How many grandbabies and what ages?" Hannah asked.

Alma began to count on her fingers. "Let's see. There's Willa and Bertie. She's named Bernice, like you, Bernice, but we call her Bertie. And then there's Jimmie, Harry, and Ben."

"I got one older grandson, he's seventeen. He wants to escort me. I said no to the twins, they're too young, and no to Celia. She wanted to be a flower girl," Bernice said. "I got no patience with kids at a time like that."

"If each of you have more than one flower girl or maid of honor, the ceremonies will take a long time, and if it's cold, that'll be hard on the folks who come to the weddings," Hannah said. "What do you all think about limiting it to either one flower girl or bridesmaid or ring bearer per couple?"

"I agree," June said. "Pick the oldest or the youngest grandchild, I say, and that way no one's feelings will get hurt. We can just tell them that's the rule."

There was more discussion, with Bernice holding out the longest, but in the end they agreed to have just one person walk down the aisle in front of the bride and her escort.

"When you get to the altar, whoever walks in front of you will sit in the front row with whoever escorts you down the aisle. The kids need to understand this, so they don't break away and go dashing off to find their parents," Hannah said.

Grace picked up from there. "After your vows, each couple will turn, walk back up the aisle, and the next couple will then start toward the altar. Who's giving you away, Bernice?"

"My father-in-law's walkin' with me. I sure wish I'd let my grandson Alden do it. He wanted to so bad, but the old man fussed so, and Ralph he just begged and begged me to let his father walk with me. We had one big fuss about it. I usually get what I want with Ralph, but that old man bothered him plenty about this. He ain't never had no daughter to give away, he keeps sayin.' So Ralph said I just had to let him do it." She heaved a deep sigh. "So finally, I said okay."

"Most of the time, that old man's too drunk to walk a straight line," June said.

"Ralph's keeping an eye on him the night before and that day, so he'll be sober," Bernice replied. "Still, I'd rather be walking with Alden. He's real tall, nearly six feet four inches. Ralph thinks he'll get a scholarship at one of them colleges in Georgia that's so big on basketball."

Hannah said, "Alden sounds like a fine young man. I can see you're very proud of him. Now, let's go on, shall we? May and Billy will be next, and then Velma and Charlie."

"Silly, I think, us acting like we was twenty," May said.

There's something unhappy about May, Grace thought. Her eyes never smile, even when her lips do. I wouldn't be surprised if that mother of hers and her sister have pressured her into this. Her heart warmed toward May.

"It's as simple as that," Hannah was saying. "And I know you'll all be happy with the flowers and decorations Amelia and Mike have planned."

"Christmas type, I hope," Bernice said. "And don't forget we gotta have a manger and the baby Jesus."

"Pastor Ledbetter's taking care of that. Everything will be there." Hannah was growing impatient. "Now, let's finish up so you can get home before it starts to snow." Grace handed her a different clipboard and she flipped through the papers. "Pastor Denny will call each of you and go over the service. I assume that you've all taken care of receptions in your own homes afterward?"

"Which pastor did you say is gonna do the marrying?" June asked.

"Pastor Denny. I doubt Pastor Johnson could stand long enough for five weddings."

The women finally bade Hannah, Grace, and Amelia good night and scurried to their cars, hugging their coats about them as they cast glances at the sky.

Hannah and Grace stood on the porch and watched them go. "It's definitely going to snow tonight. I wonder how much?" Hannah said.

"Do you think people will come to the weddings if the heat isn't fixed?" Grace asked. "Will they actually have a

Christmas Day service without heat? I feel so frustrated about all this."

"Imagine how Pastor Denny must feel. It's amazing how he carries on so cheerful and upbeat, when he's been hit with one thing after the other from the day he arrived." Hannah slipped her arm about Grace's shoulder. "You're shivering. Come on inside."

"This year it's taking me a while to make the transition from summer to fall and now winter," Grace said. "I'm liking the cold less each year. Remember when we first came here, how much warmer it felt than Pennsylvania?"

"Better start making that transition to winter fast, or you're likely to get sick. I'm just glad we all got our flu shots." Hannah closed the door and shut out the cold behind them.

"We've done all we could to help get them ready for these weddings, haven't we, Hannah?"

"In my opinion, we certainly have. We've got the procedures organized and the decorations are under control; they're handling their own invitations and receptions. With all you have to do, I'm amazed you're baking pies and cakes for Velma's reception."

"She offered to pay me, but I couldn't take money. I enjoy cooking, and I like Velma and Charlie."

"They're good folks. The more I know them, the more I like them," Hannah said. "I'm going to turn on the fireplace in the living room. What do you say we watch a movie on that new DVD player Russell got for you? I picked up some old comedies: *You Can't Take It With You* and *Harvey*. You know how to operate that machine?"

"I have the instructions written down. That's the only way I can remember from one time to the next," Grace replied. "Ask Amelia if she wants to watch with us."

A half hour later, settled snugly in their favorite chairs in the living room, they were happily watching Jimmy Stewart chat with Harvey.

18

Angry feelings were running high in the office of Covington Road Church the next day. Voices were raised, and faces set in stone. Lou Channing stood ten feet from the desk, his feet spread apart, hands shoved in his pockets, shaking his head. "It ain't gonna happen. There's not enough time."

"If you'd ordered the unit the day we gave you the order and not seven days later, it would be here and installed," Charlie said. "You got this job because you said you'd get right on it, and I especially trusted you to do just that."

"How the hell do you know I didn't get right on it?"

"I'm not stupid, Lou. I phoned your supplier in Charlotte. That unit wasn't ordered until seven days later, and you never asked for a rush on it. It's December twenty-second and I'm calling every heating contractor from here to Greenville, South Carolina, and north to Johnson City, Tennessee. Somewhere there's a heat pump and air-conditioning unit sitting in someone's shop, and we'll get it and have it installed before Christmas Eve."

"What about my unit when it gets here?" Channing's voice was angry.

"I don't much care what you do with it, Lou. You'll refund our deposit, or you'll hear from our lawyer. We've got a church to heat for the holidays. We've got five weddings Christmas Eve and a Christmas Day service, and you've let us down real bad."

"We were snowed under with work, Charlie, and then one of my kids got hurt skiing."

"You've got guys who work for you. There's no excuse," Charlie said.

"Why don't you move your services to another church?"

"Name me a church that isn't jammed with its own congregation for Christmas services," Denny said.

"Well, you ain't gonna get a heating unit this late," Channing said.

"You just wait and see." Charlie ushered Lou to the door, then turned to Denny. "I anticipated this, with his not returning your calls and all. So I've located a heating system, and I'd appreciate it if you'd get into my pickup and drive over to Erwin in Tennessee and pick it up. Erwin's a small town off to the right before you get to Johnson City. The exits to it are well marked. You take the first one. I wrote the directions down for you."

He fished in his back pants pocket and handed Denny a folded sheet of paper, then eased into a chair. "I wanted to wait to hear Channing out on this, but I called an old friend of mine, Jay Leonard, in Erwin. He's staying open, waiting for someone to come pick it up. I would go, but the way my back is, I can hardly climb into the truck. Leonard would deliver it, but his man's out sick, and his other truck's got a broken axle."

He checked his watch. "It's three now. With the new road, it should only take you about thirty minutes to get there. Jay'll have some fellows waiting to load the unit. Be sure they cover it up good. There's tarps in the back of the pickup." Charlie pulled a check from his pocket and smoothed it on the desk. "Give him this check. It's mine, but we can fix all that later." He grimaced in pain. "Sorry to put this on you, but if this thing with my back goes on much longer, I'll end up having to go into the hospital, and I want to avoid that—at least until after the wedding. Velma would kill me."

"Shouldn't you be lying down, resting? You're here all day on your feet."

"I probably should be home lying down. Well, I'll do that as soon as you're on your way. And I'm gonna call every mechanic around these parts, and find someone to install the thing when you get back no matter if it's as late as seven o'clock."

As Denny drove the pickup down Cove Road, Charlie worried that he'd made a big mistake sending the pastor off alone with the threat of snow in the air. As he limped across the road to his home, he assured himself that the pastor would be safe. Sam's Gap, at the crest of the mountain, used to be a heck of a dangerous spot before the new road was put in. People said it wasn't dangerous anymore, and with the warmer weather they'd had the last two days, any snow would probably melt as fast as it hit the ground. But just in case, he'd given Denny his cell phone.

The drive was more beautiful than Denny imagined. The old road was a narrow two-lane that twisted for eight or nine interminable miles between tall hills that blocked out the sunlight. The new highway, built high above the old road, seemed to soar through the air as birds do. Snow had obviously been falling in the higher elevations for several hours, for he saw snowcapped mountains on all sides. Lighter snow glazed the surface of the highway, which he'd heard had been constructed with new stuff in the macadam that melted the snow fast, making it safer to drive. The pickup's tires seemed to grip the road well and there was no sliding, despite the lightly falling snow.

Denny drove along at a good clip, crossed Sam's Gap, and descended into Tennessee. He soon saw the signs to Erwin and, as instructed, took the first exit. After that it was not as easy. The address Charlie had given him turned out to be incorrect. It took another fifteen minutes to locate the shop, which was outside of town on a country lane, where an impatient Mr. Leonard waited. When Denny pulled up to the door of the shop, snow was falling like a steady rain.

"I was just about to close up and go home," Jay Leonard

said. He was a tall man with wide shoulders and a thick beard.

Denny apologized. "Thank you for waiting. I got lost. I'm sorry."

As if on cue, three young men drove up in a van. They ignored Denny, ignored his cheery "Merry Christmas," and grunted as they loaded the several components of the unit into the pickup and covered them with Charlie's tarps. Then they pocketed the cash Mr. Leonard gave them, jumped into their van, and barreled away, loud music blasting.

"Better hurry home, now, Pastor," Jay Leonard said as he scratched his beard. "They're calling for a dern big storm tonight."

"The road was fine coming over."

"One thing I can guarantee you is that weather changes fast in these here parts, and the roads are about as unpredictable. One minute you'll be going along just fine, the next you're sliding off the road on a patch of black ice. Drive slow and be mighty careful, now." Mr. Leonard pocketed Charlie's check, wished Denny a Merry Christmas, and slammed the heavy metal door of his shop. The lights inside went out.

Denny was alone on an empty street facing uncertain directions on a road barely visible beneath an increasing blanket of snow. If he hadn't been able to see the tire tracks left behind by the van of the men who loaded the unit, he could have assumed that there was no road.

A great sense of loneliness swept over him, as deep as

the loneliness he had felt during so many Christmases at the orphanage. Remembering the skates that Pastor Johnson brought him for his thirteenth birthday, and how he had learned to ice-skate and been good at it, how he had loved whirling about on the ice, doing figure eights and generally showing off, lifted Denny's spirits as he drove slowly down the country road.

It took another fifteen minutes before Denny found the main street that headed toward the highway. Chilled and hungry, he stopped for coffee at a small café whose red-and-green blinking lights offered holiday cheer. Suspended from a bracket on the wall, a TV blared. A familiar weatherman's face on the Weather Channel filled the screen. Above the clatter of tables being cleared and general chatter, Denny strained to hear the man. The camera pulled back, revealing the map that showed the entire eastern seaboard colored white from Georgia to New York. Cutouts of snowflakes below dark clouds indicated snow. Denny heard the weatherman's dire prediction of a major ice and snowstorm heading east and moving fast. Suddenly frightened, he did not finish his coffee and quickly left.

The highway loomed ahead, all uphill. The few cars on it crawled along, as he did, for visibility was vastly diminished, and his windshield wipers strained to handle the swiftly accumulating snow.

Denny punched in Charlie's number on the cell phone. No answer. He called the parsonage. No answer. Good Lord, had something happened to Pastor Johnson? He dialed Grace's number.

After several rings, Amelia picked up the phone. "You sound so far away. Where are you?" she asked.

"On the highway, almost to the top of Sam's Gap."

"Why are you out in such terrible weather?"

"I went to Erwin in Tennessee to pick up a heating unit for the church. It's in the back of the pickup, Charlie's pickup." Crackling noises intervened. Denny shouted into the phone, "Can you hear me?"

"Barely. But yes, go ahead."

"Please let Charlie Herrill know I'm on my way home." His windshield wipers squealed, protesting the thick, wet snow that fell faster than they could remove it. "If I can see to get home, that is."

"There's a welcome station not far from where you are, on the right. Pull in there and wait this storm out," Amelia said. "If you don't hit someone, someone could smash into you. The weatherman says it's an all-night affair, and the roads are getting icy down here. They must be iced over up there, or they will be any minute."

"You're probably right. It's pretty awful driving. I'll do that. I can't reach Pastor Johnson by phone. Will you call for me, make sure he's all right? Thanks."

This is some mess I'm in, Denny thought. His foot felt heavy on the brake as he inched along, squinting to stay in his lane, to see any car or truck alongside or ahead of him. When he occasionally picked up the glare of red tail-lights, he offered a prayer of thanks. He thought about cause, effect, and consequences, and for a moment felt angry with Pastor Johnson for not raising the alarm a year ago about the antiquated furnace. The next instant he regretted those thoughts. Still, Johnson ought to have retired years ago and turned the affairs of the church over to a younger man. *Stop this! What ifs and ought tos serve no purpose. He's old and frail and did what he could.* A gust of wind caused the solid pickup to wobble. *Where is that welcome station?*

The situation continued to deteriorate at a rate that astounded him. One instant he could discern a mountain, the next it was invisible. His concern increased by the moment. In the murk and slush, he nearly missed the turnoff to the welcome station and came inches shy of hitting the rear end of a car easing its way ahead of him. It was now five-thirty in the afternoon, and without the glow issuing from bright lights on tall poles in the parking lot, Denny would not have located the building.

Cars, vans, and trucks of various sizes crowded the lot, and he drove like a tortoise until the pickup's tires slipped off the pavement and sank into mushy soil. In shoes not fit for such weather, Denny trudged through the ankle-deep snow, past parked vehicles and clumps of people, dark forms hunched against the wind, inching their way toward the building. Inside the welcome center, a huge stone fireplace warmed visitors. Early arrivals occupied every available seat. Small children lay on the rugs; babies in car seats and strollers cried. Denny located an empty spot against a wall and eased himself to the floor. He sat with his legs drawn to his chest, his head back against the wall.

Men stood at the glass panes as if their looking out

would affect the rate of snowfall, while women tended the best they could to the needs of their families, and several park service employees hastened back and forth to an office behind the high counter with trays of coffee, tea, and soft drinks.

"Please, God, don't let the power go out. That fireplace alone will never be able to heat this room," said a large, grizzled man with a short-cropped beard and tattoos on his arms.

A trucker or a biker, Denny thought, until a little girl of about six ran up to the man and clutched his leg.

"I'm scared, Daddy." The man swung her to his hip and kissed her cheek tenderly.

"Don't be scared, Iris," he said. "God has sent his angels to bring the snow and make the world extra special pretty for us, and He's given us this nice warm room to watch it from."

Shamed by his rush to judgment, Denny added his prayers to the man's. He tried the cell phone, which emitted a faint beep. The battery was fading. He accepted a cup of coffee from an overworked-looking young woman. It was weak, probably watered to stretch availability, but it felt good going down. Thank God he was off the road and warm.

A child somewhere in the room began to cry, loud piercing wails that awakened several of the sleeping children. Soon a cacophony of crying filled the room. Flustered mothers looked apologetically around as they attempted to quiet and comfort their youngsters. An older woman, who appeared to be alone, put both hands over her ears and moved to the farthest corner of the room. She looked as if any minute she would cry, too.

Denny thought of how quiet the snow-blanketed world outside must be, and of Marguerite's thick fur hat, the kind Russians wore in the movies, and if a hat like that, covering one's ears as hers had, would act as a sound barrier, as well as a barrier against the cold. He closed his eyes. Lord, how he wished he were home with Bill Johnson in the snug parsonage.

The next thing he knew, someone tapped his shoulder. Denny opened his eyes to a room almost devoid now of noise or people. The tired-looking park service lady asked, "Are you all right? It's stopped snowing. The plows are clearing the road. Nearly everyone's gone."

Denny lifted and lowered each shoulder and rolled his neck. "I can leave?"

"Yes. Do you want some coffee or a soft drink before you go?"

"A Coke, please, if you've got one."

"There are a few left. We stock for emergencies."

"Do they happen often?"

"We can count on several severe storms like this each winter," she said.

"My pickup," Denny said, remembering. "My tires went off the paved parking area. I'm not sure I can get it out."

"Manny will help you. He's just come on duty."

A young man, short but solid, with biceps indicating he worked out regularly, appeared. Manny extended his hand.

"Help you up, sir?" His grip was strong, and Denny was on his feet in a moment.

"Thanks, I appreciate it. I'm stiff all over."

"I imagine you would be. Long night. You're lucky you could sleep through all the kids crying and the storm. At least it went through the area fast."

"Some of those kids never went to sleep," the woman said. "It gets on your nerves after a while, no matter how understanding you try to be."

Outside, the sky was clear and brilliant blue. Plows had piled the snow in hills about the parking lot and along the sides of the highway. With Manny's help, the pickup eased back onto the pavement and Denny was off. God was present everywhere in the pristine beauty surrounding him, and Denny felt that he could reach out with his fingertips and touch the mountains. He thought of the burly man he'd thought was a biker and little Iris. God's angels had done a superb job. His heart rejoiced at the loveliness, the gift of the day, and then he remembered it was December 23.

Alone, with time to think as he descended the mountain, Denny's attention drifted to the weddings. He was apprehensive about performing five, one after the other, and making each one special. Should they have separated the weddings? He also wasn't sure that he could carry on with a Christmas Eve service after conducting five weddings. Painting the church, heating the church, weddings, Christmas services—everything jammed together like this was just too much.

Cars lined Cove Road in front of the church. Denny pulled into the drive and parked by the basement entrance. Inside the church hall, a meeting that included council members, the wedding couples, and the three ladies was in session, and he was greeted with hugs from the women and pats on the back from the men.

"We were worried sick about you," Grace said.

"Baptism by snow and ice, eh, Pastor?" Frank Craine said. "One thing you learn in these parts: always keep one eye and one ear out for the weather."

"I'm gonna get you a weather radio," Velma said.

Wrapped in a heavy jacket, a thick wool hat pulled close about his face, Pastor Johnson hugged him hard. "I prayed for you, son. Charlie and Velma came over and got me; they insisted I stay at their place. Guess they worried I'd freeze to death if the heat in the parsonage went off."

Worn out and bleary eyed from squinting into the glare of sun on snow, Denny had never been so glad to see them all. He pulled the receipt for the heating unit from his pocket and laid it on the table.

"You did good, Denny." Charlie held the receipt over his head. "Denny here got us our heat pump!"

Everyone clapped, and someone whistled approval.

"And we got a mechanic who's gonna install it," Billy McCorkle said. "Ralph's got a friend, Jake Henderson from Tryon, down the mountain. He's coming up to put in that unit for us soon as Ralph phones him. Jake's a good man, very reliable. Ralph says if Jake says he'll be somewhere, he's there right on the button."

Hannah appeared with a cup of coffee for Denny, and Grace trailed her with cream, sugar, and her famous sugar cookies on a tray.

Charlie said, "Sorry I sent you off like that, Pastor. Guess I didn't pay no attention to the weather, either."

"It was quite an adventure, but thank the Lord, it turned out well." Denny was glad to be home, home in Covington, home with these friends.

By noon of December 23, Eddy McCorkle squeezed past the big blue truck parked in the church's driveway. He popped into the pastor's office and whispered, "Is it done yet?"

Denny had asked Amelia and Hannah, for Grace was busy cooking, to take shifts in his office to answer the phone and fend off questions that might come in.

"Not done yet," Amelia replied. "Soon." She hadn't a clue when soon might be, but that answer seemed to satisfy those who inquired.

Eddy hunted down Denny and stood in the cold beside him to watch as old Jake and his son, Freddie, struggled to get the air compressor down from the back of the pickup, load it onto a dolly, and ease it onto a makeshift pad a few feet away from the church.

Eddy and Denny stood side by side in silence for a long time before Eddy said, "I'll be off then." He rubbed his gloved hands together and departed, leaving Denny alone to watch anxiously as Jake and his son carried the air handler to the basement. He listened to the banging and shoving, a yell now and then as one man called to another, a grunt, a swear word. Then Freddie emerged, grim faced, and without a word climbed into his truck and drove away.

"He's going for a part we need," Jake said.

Denny had not heard him or seen him emerge from the building. The old man looked tired. "Come on in for some coffee, won't you?" Denny asked.

"Nah. I got a thermos, and I still got work to do." In a moment Jake was gone and Denny was alone again, worrying whether supply stores would be open two days before Christmas, and assuring himself that of course they would be. Denny wandered back to the parsonage to update Pastor Johnson.

Moments later, Jake appeared in the office. He was ancient, how old Amelia could not guess, and bowlegged and bent, and the stubble on his chin was probably a week old. Amelia offered him a chair. He eased himself into it and removed his cap. His thin gray hair was pressed flat and the cap had left a red rim across his forehead. She offered him a cup of coffee, which he declined. Moments later, Denny appeared. Amelia rose and pointed him to his seat behind the desk. "I'm going out for a few minutes," she said.

Jake looked at Denny and shook his head. "Pastor, looks like we got a problem. The new air handler won't fit the old ducts."

After all this, were they going to have no heat?

Jake continued. "I sent my boy to get some large flexible

duct, so we can jury-rig a connection between the new unit and the old duct and give you heat for the holidays. Afterward, I'll make a permanent transition piece."

Denny understood nothing the old man said, but he trusted him. He had no choice. "Thank you. I appreciate all the work you and Freddie are doing, especially before Christmas."

"Gonna try our darnedest. You get into that there church now and pray Freddie gets what we need."

After working for hours to connect the old system to the new one, Jake and his son finally finished. "We'll be back tomorrow morning good and early to test this," he said.

At six-thirty A.M. on Christmas Eve, Denny awoke to the sound of a truck door slamming. The knock on the front door snapped him out of bed. From his room, Pastor Johnson called, "Are there problems?"

"I hope not," Denny called back. "It's the men installing the new heating system. They're finishing up today."

There was a loud knock on the door again, and Denny hastened to open it.

"Pastor." Freddie's deep voice boomed from the doorway. "We're gonna turn on the unit now. We need you to go inside the church and check to see if the heat's coming up all right. If it's working okay, you got to get all the vents open so the church'll warm up before those weddings."

Denny jabbed his legs into sweatpants and his feet into

his running shoes, pulled a sweatshirt over his long-sleeved T-shirt, grabbed a cinnamon roll, and sprinted to the church.

At each dark brown vent he squatted and rested his hand over it, grateful each time a gentle stir of warm air touched his fingers. With every vent he checked, he dashed to the top of the basement stairs and yelled, "Another one working fine."

From below, as from a deep cavern, came old Jake's voice, "Well, good!"

And Denny raced back to locate another vent, and another, and another. The ceiling was peaked and high—it would take forever to heat this space. Still, it was better to have a temperature of fifty-five or sixty than the thirty-six degrees the thermometer read outside the parsonage door.

After one of his declarations that another vent was working, the voice below said, "Be sure all the doors in the church are closed off, so no hot air's gonna escape." Then Jake directed him to check the vents in the vestibule, the meeting hall, and his office, and to close off each room. It was nine A.M. before Denny called down, "Everything's working beautifully, thank God."

"Well, good!" came the reply. "Meet us in your office. I'll go over everything you need to know about this system."

A half hour later, Denny had been given a manual and was instructed to read it carefully and slowly several times. Jake showed him where several separate controls were.

"This'll give you better coverage," he said. "This way,

you can work in a nice warm office without having to heat the whole church when it's not in use. You're all set now, so we'll be heading home. Have a good Christmas, and I hope all those weddings come off okay."

Denny shook Jake's thick, callused hand. "Merry Christmas and thank you, again." Moments later he heard their truck doors slam, and they were gone. He hastened back to the parsonage to share the good news.

19

The wallpaper in June's bedroom clung to the wall with a desperation born of old age. It had been there since before her first child was born, thirty-nine years ago. She had fallen in love at first sight with the paper, a busy jumble of flowers in various shades of yellow, orange, mauve, and pink. From the day it went up, Eddy complained that it hurt his eyes and made him dizzy. June still loved it. She loved lying in bed on a Sunday morning and separating and counting the flowers according to size and color. She never got the same number twice, but that didn't bother her.

When Eddy fussed about the busyness of the paper, she suggested that he close his eyes. Soon his favorite way of teasing her was to shut his eyes when he entered the room, especially at night, stiff arms out in front of him like Frankenstein. It was interesting that he never tripped over anything.

She was sure he peeped, for the things he bumped into

seemed to be carefully selected: an end table without a lamp on it, the back of the armchair over which she laid out her clothes for the next day. If she was almost asleep he would bump into the bedpost, not hard enough to jolt her, just enough to get her attention.

Today Eddy was dressed an hour ahead of her and waited down in the sitting room. Every few minutes he called up to June, "You getting ready? You painting a picture or what?"

She hadn't been able to eat lunch, what with being as nervous as a girl. In two hours they had to be at the church. But June's nervousness was a controlled nervousness, nothing like the hubbub that arrived when Ida bustled into her bedroom with May in tow.

Her mother's new dress, bought especially for this occasion, was too blue, too bright, too garish, especially since Ida had insisted on giving June away. She wanted to scream. Ida would upstage any bride if she wore that dress. Where had she gotten it and when?

"That's a pretty dress, Mama, but it seems to me you got to wear a dress that matches better with my suit. May and I are both wearing lighter colors."

Ida ignored her. "I told May to fix the collar on that suit of hers. It ain't lying flat. She should have ironed it. Why didn't you iron it, May?"

May looked overwrought, close to tears. She reached up and repeatedly flattened the offending collar with the palm of her hand. "It'll have to do. I got no time to iron it now."

"June's got an iron. I could get the board and set it up right here."

"May looks fine, and don't change the subject on me." June said. "If you wear that dress, you'll take all the attention from us brides. Please, Mama, wear something lighter colored. If you went home now, or we left a bit early and stopped at your place, you could change quick enough."

Ida ignored June again and circled May, checking her from top to bottom as if she were five years old. "Well, the best you can do then is to keep pressing that collar down with your hand. Maybe it'll flatten by the time you walk down the aisle." Her nose wrinkled as she studied her daughter's hair. "I don't much like the way that beauty parlor woman done your hair. Puttin' it up like that makes you look way older than June."

May's eyes grew teary. Her hands reached for the curls the beautician at Lily's Salon had pulled back and lifted high on her head. She thought they were lovely. "I can't do nothing right for you, can I, Mama?"

"Mama," June said. "Why you saying these things to May? Her suit's so pretty no one's gonna notice her collar, and I think her hair looks good."

Ida was adamant. "Her hair ain't good. It's too fussy. I coulda done it better for her myself."

"Then fix it for me, Mama," May said.

Ida proceeded to take the pins out of May's hair and brush the curls out. She twisted the shoulder-length hair and wound it in a knot atop May's head. May looked at herself in the mirror and burst into tears. "It looks worse, Mama. Fix it for me, June."

"Mama," June said, "you go downstairs and see to it

that Eddy's tie's on right, and if it ain't, you fix it for me, would you, please? And see that he eats something—not sweets, what with his diabetes and all." She turned to May. "Now don't you worry none, honey." June brushed her sister's hair. "It's so pretty brushed out like this. I'll just use the curling iron and flip up the ends, and it'll be really smart."

May smoothed her collar with nervous strokes of her hand. "Sometimes Mama makes me so mad. Seems to me, she's more nervous than either one of us." May caught sight of herself in the mirror. "Oh, look what crying's done to my face. I gotta wash off this makeup and put it on again. I *hate* makeup."

"You go ahead and wash your face, and I'll put it back on fresh for you."

"You were always so good at making yourself pretty. When we were growing up, I envied you, June."

"But you wouldn't let me touch your face then," June remembered. "Not even when Billy came courtin'."

A shiver passed through May. How could she ever have let herself get so enamored of Billy McCorkle? Ida had warned her about the McCorkles.

"Don't you go gettin' yourself hooked up with no McCorkle. They don't make good husbands," she'd said. "And you gotta live back up there at McCorkle Creek with all his kin."

So look what had happened. Both her daughters had married McCorkles, and Ida fit in with her in-laws and their kin better than May and even June did.

June set about repairing her sister's makeup, after which the sisters complimented each other's hair, makeup, and clothes. May's pantsuit, chosen by June, was a lovely shade of teal and brought out the green of her eyes. June looked smart in a soft rose-colored outfit.

They surveyed themselves in the full-length mirror. "Why, May, don't we look as pretty as a flower garden? Now you don't worry none, honey. We'll have us a good old time today, and we're gonna be the prettiest of the five brides. We're the youngest, too, only fifty-eight. You remember back when that minister Simms married the five of us couples one day after the other, like he was in a big hurry?"

"He was in a big hurry. He knew it was only a question of time and he'd be found out," May said. "He used to flirt with me. I never told nobody that."

"Well, my gosh, he did the same to me," her sister said. "I put him in his place, gave him a good swift kick in the shins one day when he actually tried to put his arm around me."

"Maybe that's why he got kicked out of seminary. Maybe he got involved with some married woman."

"I wonder if he hit on Bernice, too?" June said.

"I'm sure not going to ask her. She'd chew my head off, probably." May busied herself flattening her collar, buttoning and unbuttoning the top two buttons of her suit. "June, I gotta ask you something. Don't be mad at me now, okay?"

"When do I ever get mad at you?"

"Well, this is something big that might make you mad."

"I won't get mad. What is it?"

"Would you marry Eddy again if you were starting over young?" May bit her lip. "I wouldn't marry Billy again if I was young. Maybe that's why I'm so edgy, and why it's so hard to have Mama nagging at me about every little thing. I almost feel sometimes she can read my mind."

"Mama can't read no minds, but she's shrewd. She tries to get people's goat. She'll tell them something she knows isn't true, because she knows people will overreact and tell her exactly what she wants to know. I've seen it work time and again. It works with you. I'm surprised you haven't figured it out by now."

May turned away from her sister to collect herself and stop the tears forming behind her eyelids. What June said about Mama was true, and over the years she had schooled herself not to react, especially when anything came up about Billy or Billy and herself. But now May was about to confess to her sister the truth about her life with Billy, a truth she had kept hidden all these years. "There are days I want to run away just so's not to have to marry Billy. If I left before the wedding, I'd be free."

June took a step back and stared at May.

"Now don't go getting mad at me," May said.

"I'm not mad, just surprised. No, I'm shocked. What do you mean free, May?" She shook her head. "What does that mean, when you've got four grown kids with families? You'd be running out on them, too, and they're not even legitimate yet, according to what Charlie Herrill says. You got to marry Billy, for the kids' and your grandkids' sake."

May slumped against the bedpost of June's large bed and her mouth quivered at the corners. "I know all that. I've been unhappy with Billy most of this marriage. If I left, I wouldn't have to go on pretending our life together is good. I wouldn't have to go on putting up with his crap."

June's voice showed her hurt. "But you never said nothing to me."

"I never did to nobody. Mama warned me about marrying Billy, and she'd never let me forget it. As it turned out, after we got married I didn't like Billy, and Mama did. They drank beer together, and watched ball games, and had them a good old time. And I had the kids. Joey was a handful, if you remember. Always getting in trouble at school, fighting, and then getting picked up by the cops for speeding more than one time. I couldn't handle him alone, and I didn't think I could take care of the lot of them by myself.

"Yet I can't stop thinking about what I'm doing now. Why I don't love Billy. I don't even like him. I hate all the years I never told you the truth, and I hate everything about my life with Billy."

"Good heavens, May. I'm sorry. Why'd you wait so late to tell me all this?" June started toward her sister, arms outstretched, but May stepped back.

"I been ashamed, I guess, but now I feel I gotta say this out. Through the years I blamed myself, getting pregnant like that and all. I figured it was my fault I wasn't happy. I thought maybe I wasn't saying or doing the right thing to make Billy happy." She clasped her hands before her. "Nothing I ever did made me or Billy happy, June. Nothing at all, and nothing he does makes me happy." Tears filled her eyes. "There never was a more mismatched couple. He's had other women. One time I followed him all the way over to West Asheville, and I saw her. What a floozy. Just like prostitutes you see in the movies—a short hiked-up skirt, all kinds of jewelry and makeup. It made me sick. That's when I stopped sleeping with him."

"You should have told me. Maybe Eddy could have talked to him. Now, don't you go crying again." June sank into the chair at her vanity. "I don't know what to say to you, May. It's late to bring this up, what with the men all dressed and waiting to go, and the weddings planned." She shook her head. "I can't believe you haven't said a word in all these years."

"See, you're mad at me."

"I'm not mad at you. I feel hurt you didn't tell me. I thought we told each other everything." June stood and lifted her head and shoulders in a firm gesture. "Seems to me you got to go ahead with this wedding. Afterward you could make a plan to leave him, decide where you'll live and how you're gonna support yourself. But I don't think you got a choice now because of the children, if nothing else, May."

May heaved a deep sigh and shook her head. "I have no plan to leave Billy until I got my own money."

June said, "I'm sorry about all this, but what's done is done. At least Billy don't hit you, like some men do their wives. You must have found some kind of way to live with him all these years, or you'd have lost your mind."

There had been times when May had thought she *would*

lose her mind. Besides his infidelities and his cheap nature–
the way he doled out money, questioned everything she
bought, every can of food, every pair of shoes for the kids–
she had plenty of reasons to dislike her husband. He often
pretended not to hear when she asked him or told him
something, and then said that she'd never said it. That
about drove her nuts. After May saw an old black-and-white
movie on TV called *Gaslight,* about a man who was deter-
mined to make his wife think she was going crazy, she had a
name for how she felt. "Gaslighted" was exactly how she felt
when Billy denied her reality. "Sometimes we don't have
choices. I guess, for me, this is one of those times. You've
been lucky with Eddy, June."

June nodded and thanked the Lord. She'd been mad for
Eddy and still was. One thing they loved to do was talk;
Lord, they talked about every little thing. The thought of
May leaving, maybe moving out of the area, scared and sad-
dened June. Except for May, she had no close girlfriends.
She had never needed any–not with Eddy being her best
friend, and her sister right down the street. She and Eddy
did everything together: shopped for his clothes and her
clothes, grocery shopped, and except for the wallpaper, they
had picked out all their furnishings together.

Every Easter vacation, when the children were little,
they had taken them down to Carowind Park in Charlotte,
and when they got older and no longer wanted to go, June
and Eddy went anyway. They loved all the rides, even the
high roller coaster that scared June to pieces. She'd grab
hold of Eddy and hang on for dear life. These days they

took their grandchildren. Yes, her life with Eddy had been fun and generally a happy one. She felt terrible for May.

May was asking, "You'd marry Eddy again if you were young, wouldn't you?"

"Yes, of course I would."

By turning the conversation away from herself, May began to regain her composure. June was right, of course. Over the years she had not planned well, had not gone to school or learned a trade. She had never worked outside her home, had had no money to put aside. She had been overcome with a great inertia, and playacting that she was fine took all the strength she could muster. May knew that she had boxed herself into a corner. She had lived a lie for so long, it was easier for her to carry on than to make any changes.

"Anything you'd do different?" she asked June.

June walked over to May and hugged her. "Sure, there are things I'd have done different. Who wouldn't? I'd of liked to have had fewer children. Two would have done fine instead of four. I'd have liked to have gone to AB Tech and taken classes so I could work in a dentist's office. But no, I ain't sorry I married Eddy. He's been a good husband and father, and he's taken good care of us."

May said, "One thing's for sure: after this is over, no matter what Billy says, I'm going to work part-time. I'm going to start to make a life for myself. If older women like Grace and Hannah and Amelia can change their lives, then I can, too. And after I've saved some money, I'm moving out."

June was surprised by her sister's forceful tone. "Work where, doing what? Move where?"

"I don't know yet. Miss Lurina lives alone; maybe she'd rent me a room. She could use having someone in that house with her. As for work . . ." May's face grew animated for the first time since she had arrived at June's house. "I met this lady. She's bought old Mrs. Sheely's little house, the one over in Weaverville we always admired, with the pretty decorations around the porch. Well, she's painted it up nice, and she's opening a shop to sell old-time things like quilts and spinning wheels, tools no one uses no more but some folks collect, and jams and jellies, and candies like we used to get when we were kids. I'd have to wear a long skirt and an apron. It's kind of a costume, she said, for atmosphere, and use an old-time cash register, which suits me fine and—"

"May! June!" Ida's foghorn voice beckoned them downstairs.

June put her arm around her sister and squeezed her shoulder. "I think it's great, you going to work. You'll have money of your own. You'll tell me more about your plans later, promise?"

20

Before leaving for the church, Charlie sneaked up behind Velma, slipped his arms about her, and kissed her neck. "You look mighty pretty, sweetheart. You're gonna be the prettiest bride walking down that aisle today."

Her eyes traveled the length of him. "And the oldest. But look at you—don't you look right handsome yourself?"

"Before we found out we weren't married," he said, "I'd been thinking it would be nice to renew our wedding vows like some folks are doing these days."

"That would have been nice. You know, Charlie, every time I think about Simms not being ordained and going ahead like he did and marrying us, and Griffen Anson not telling anyone, it makes me mad. But then I think this has been fun, preparing for our wedding like I was a girl again, and the grandkids so excited. Megan's thrilled she's gonna walk in front of us and throw flower petals. Amelia promised to give her a whole basketful. It's something that child will remember all her life, don't you think?"

"I think so. She's seven, old enough to remember. But I still say you look like a girl yourself."

His words warmed her. "That's silly, but thanks anyway."

He brought out a small velvet box from his pocket. "I bought us new rings, honey."

Velma opened the box. The rings were bright, shiny gold, and wider than the band she'd worn for forty years. She worked the original gold band up and squeezed hard to get it over the knuckle of her finger, then studied the light circle it left behind on her finger. "I declare. Who'd have thought it would be so hard to get off?" The new ring went on easily. "You got this one larger. How'd you know I'd need a bigger size, Charlie?"

"I had trouble getting mine off, so I figured you would, too."

She studied the new rings. "It's wider. I like it wider."

"Look inside," Charlie said.

Velma smiled at the ease with which the new band slid off her finger. "Why, Charlie, you old romantic." She read aloud, "'Velma and Charlie. Love is forever.' That's so sweet." She kissed him. "This is such fun, isn't it?"

"It's a bit nerve-racking, thinking about walking down the aisle again, an old goat like me."

"A randy old goat, too," she said, and reached out to tickle him.

He stopped her hand. "Don't get me going now, Velma, honey. Or we'll never make it to the church."

She handed him back the new ring, which he placed in the box alongside his. "It would look stupid if I forgot to take this off now, and I had to take it off at the altar so you could put it on again, wouldn't it?"

He snapped the small box shut and slipped it into his inside jacket pocket, then took a three-by-five card out and his pen. Turning from her, he began to write something.

Velma gathered up her hat and veil. "Charlie, what are you doing?"

"Adding something to what I'm gonna say to you at the altar."

"You've scribbled away on that card for days now. What are you going to say? Show me." She reached for the card.

He stepped back and shoved the card into his pocket. "None of that, now. We said we'd surprise each other. Have I asked you to tell me what you've written?"

"No, but you know it's not going to be something that's gonna make you laugh right up there in front of the pastor and everyone."

He grinned. "Let's go."

Velma looked about her, making sure she'd forgotten nothing. "A lot of good things have come out of this whole business, Charlie. For one thing, it's helped take Miss Lurina's mind off the loss of Old Man, and another good thing is that it's brought Alma and me closer to Grace, Hannah, and Amelia. I never knew Amelia much. She's a nice person, and she's funny. I used to think she was a little crazy."

"She's probably the most unusual of those three ladies, wouldn't you say?"

"That's right. She's very creative. I sneaked into the church last night, and my, it's beautiful with the flowers Amelia and her friend Mike fixed for us. And that French lady sent red roses for the table. Can you imagine, Charlie, dozens of red roses in wintertime? Must have cost her a small fortune."

"She's been very generous to our church. Denny said she had tea with them before she left and she writes to Pastor Johnson regularly." Charlie took his wife's arm. "Want me to drive us over?"

She kissed his cheek lightly. "You're a dear, but goodness, no. It's just across the road. But hold on to my arm real tight—I'm not used to these high heels, and I don't want to twist an ankle or take a tumble on the steps. How does your back feel?"

He reached behind him. "With this brace the doctor gave me and the muscle-relaxing pills, I'm okay. He says I'm going to have to go for physical therapy twice a week once the wedding's over." He offered her his arm again. "You ready, sweetheart?"

Velma bent closer to the mirror for one last look and dabbed powder on her nose. "Now, I'm ready."

In the house next door to the Herrills', Alma stood in front of the full-length wall mirror in the upstairs bedroom. The room was larger than it had been in the old farmhouse, and reminded her of a solarium with its many windows to the southeast. Sunshine flooded it most of the day. Her carefully tended plants used to die for want of light, but now her new Christmas cactus and other plants thrived on a stand near a window.

Trying to see how her yellow dress looked from the back, Alma twisted to the right and to the left. Did this light color and the fullness of the skirt make her rear end look too big? She had stepped on her bathroom scale this morning, and to her great distress found that she had gained two pounds, even with dieting these last few days. Maybe she should have listened to Velma and bought a nice suit in a dark color. It was wintertime, after all, and this dress was rather frilly and youthful. Alma smoothed the skirt. Well, it was too late—what was done was done.

Frank, in his new blue suit, called from downstairs. "Don't keep me waiting long. I know how you can fuss and primp in front of that mirror."

He looked so good, just like when they'd married the first time. She liked it that at seventy he was still a handsome man, that he kept his body in good shape, no paunch, almost no flab anywhere. Coaching football had seen to that. Frank coached when their boys were little and right through high school. Now he was occupied with the grandkids, taking them swimming at the gym in Asheville and coaching Little League. Frank also played softball on a senior team on Sunday afternoons and did push-ups regularly. All this put a burden on Alma to keep her weight down and look her best.

When she'd snagged Frank, the girls with whom she'd worked at the Atlas plant over in Enka went green with envy. Frank was older by six years and her supervisor. He'd flirted with her for weeks, until, with prodding from the other girls, she'd plucked up her courage and sat down at his table in the cafeteria. He'd liked her spunk, he told her later.

Alma patted a stray strand of hair back into place and reached for the hair spray. Before spraying, she closed her eyes. How she'd floated down that church aisle forty years ago, everyone admiring her, admiring them as a couple. She'd considered herself the gosh-darn luckiest girl in the world. Not that she hadn't had her share of ups and downs; who could be married forty years and not have good times and bad times? No marriage was perfect. For one thing, Frank never stopped flirting with women, and to this very day, all these years later and at their ages, she still didn't trust him out of her sight.

"Once a flirt, always a flirt," her mother had said. "Just look at those bedroom eyes he's got, like a movie star. If you marry him, you make up your mind to live with it."

His flirting just about drove Alma crazy. Jealousy just about drove her crazy.

And then to top it all, though he had promised her a home of their own, they up and moved in with his anxiety-ridden mother and his commonplace, colorless father on Cove Road.

"My mother's still grieving my brother's death in the war. She'll get over it in time. This is just for a while," Frank said to her on their honeymoon. "Then we'll get us a place of our own." At that time, she could deny him nothing.

Alma soon discovered that losing Frank's younger

brother in Korea had left his mother fearful of life itself. Distrustful of her husband, whom she considered a philanderer and a poor provider, she hung on Frank, doted on Frank. Maybe that's why he stayed at the Enka plant until it closed its doors. His mama felt "right proud" that he was a manager there, and he'd waited until after she passed to open that auto parts store he'd dreamed of for so many years.

"Frank, your father don't look well," his mother would say at least twice a week. "Frank, it looks like we gonna have a flood in the backyard and the corn's gonna drown."

The corn gave a bumper crop that year.

"Frank, I don't like the sound of that new truck your father bought. It's all them fancy new things it's got on it, like telling how cold or hot it is outside from inside the car. That don't seem natural. Stuff like that draws from what it takes to run a car. Ain't you noticed the truck don't run right?" She had refused to ride in it.

That truck ran just fine for the next five years.

And on and on, year after year. Every year when school started, the kids would catch a cold, which Alma considered normal. Mother Craine walked around wringing her hands, looking as if someone had died. "I hear tell a bad fever's going around. If the boys get it, it could addle their brains."

It was always something with the boys, especially Harley. Maybe she oughtn't have given him that name, it being old-fashioned, and the boys teased him at school. He was too thin, too tall for his age, too quiet, Anne complained. Her other two grandsons weren't quiet *enough* to suit the old woman, and she would go around holding her hands over her ears when they came dashing into the house after the school bus dropped them off. Always something. She'd yell at them plenty, and after a time, the kids paid their Granny no mind. But she loved them, bless her heart, and God forbid anyone outside their family said a bad word about any of them.

"Anne Craine won't live forever," Alma's mother had said. "Frank makes a good living. Staying with his folks, you can save money. You got you three fine boys. We've all got troubles. I had my share with your pa, rest his soul. Anne Craine's a cross you just gotta bear."

Alma learned to accept her mother-in-law. She never did learn to cook real good, because the older woman held sway over the kitchen and could cook up a pot of beans, fry chicken, and make the best corn bread you ever ate. And there were other advantages to a live-in grandmother. Alma could pretty much go and come as she pleased. She had had, perhaps, too much free time on her hands.

"You watch yourself, now," her mother said. "Idle hands tempt the devil."

Perhaps that was why Alma had focused so much of her energy on Frank's attentions to other women—the way he smiled at them, pulled out their chairs, made them feel special. He claimed it was all harmless courtesy. She found his behavior toward other women humiliating. To counter this, she worked hard at looking her best, and as the years passed, at looking younger. She spent hours every week at the gym working out, keeping a trim figure. She colored her hair, painted her nails, and had her teeth whitened when they began to yellow. To keep the romance alive in their marriage, Alma dragged a reluctant Frank on cruises: the Panama Canal, the Caribbean, Alaska, the Bahamas, Mexico, and back to the Caribbean. She bought sexy black nightgowns and feigned sexual interest to meet his needs and keep him happy.

It hadn't been easy. Her insecurity narrowed her vision, made her picky and critical, and she knew it. She had only one friend, Velma, and they had become friends because they were neighbors, because their sons played together, and because Velma was big boned and wide hipped and Frank never flirted with her. Besides, Frank always had great respect for Charlie. For years, they'd watched the Sunday ball games together at one of their houses.

Alma's attention returned to the present when her daughter-in-law, Susan, six months pregnant, knocked lightly, then opened the door. "Dad's waiting downstairs. He's getting antsy. Don't you look lovely! That's a great color for you, that yellow."

Susan and Tommy already had two children and now her belly bulged with a baby. Alma laughed. "Here I am getting married to the baby's grandpa, making it all legal."

Still, not being legally married to Frank had not made the slightest difference in her life, had it? She'd come to believe that the Lord had his ways. She had prayed for daughters, and the Lord had seen fit to send her three fine, strapping sons. She had wanted to live closer to Asheville, where she could see lights and get a sense of life and activity. She had never liked the darkness and the quiet of the country, and here she was still. She had certainly never anticipated living with Frank's folks until four years ago, when first the old man, and six weeks later her mother-in-law, passed away. Frank had cried like a baby when his mother died. Alma had pretended to cry and had covered her eyes with a handkerchief.

There'd always been, deep inside her, a suppressed urge to kick up her heels and chuck convention. Looking back, she believed she'd married too young and tolerated too much crap from his mother and from Frank himself. She had listened to her mother, adjusted and conformed, and in so doing set herself up as the authority by which things ought to be done, like wearing a hat with a brim no more than eight inches wide and no higher than four inches. She was never late, not for anything, and she criticized and fumed about anyone who was. Alma always dressed properly in stockings and heels, even to go to the grocery. Everyone ought to! You never knew who you'd meet, or if you'd take sick and have to be carried off to the hospital. That quirk, she thought, looking back, probably came from living so long with that neurotic Anne Craine.

Perhaps because of Frank's liking them so much, Alma grew to dislike women. She mastered "the look" and could give another woman such a withering glare, up and down, that the object of her scorn would stutter and blush, and Alma would go away feeling satisfied. She prayed to God for forgiveness for this behavior, especially as sometimes she did it without provocation, just for the fun of it. Frank said that's why they hardly got asked to anyone's home. And that's why, when the ladies first came to Covington, he had insisted that they go to their picnic out under that old oak that had survived the fire. Alma enjoyed watching the English sitcom with Hyacinth Bouquet, *Keeping Up Appearances*. Hyacinth amused her. She knew exactly how Hyacinth's mind worked and why she did what she did.

But today's a new beginning. I've made me a promise not to make other women feel small, not to open my mouth to criticize, or cut someone with my eyes. Everyone's been so nice about these weddings. No one's been mean-mouthed about it. I've got me a new attitude; I just got to keep reminding myself.

Alma studied herself one last time in the full-length mirror. The yellow chiffon was pretty, and she was glad she had bought it. To heck with what Velma or anyone else thought. "I'm ready," she called.

21

❧

December 24 dawned clear and sunny, with blue skies and hardly a breeze to ruffle the brides' new hairdos. It was forty-three degrees at seven A.M., fifty degrees at noon, and fifty-seven degrees at two P.M. All along Cove Road, holiday decorations created a festive air that quite suited the day: greenery wound about porch railings, red ribbons on porch posts and mailboxes, and Christmas trees set up in yards and decorated with bright red bows and silver ornaments.

Before heading for the church, Grace stepped outside to check the tree Bob had set up on their lawn a few days ago, and to which he and his grandchildren, Tyler and Melissa, were adding last-minute decorations. With her rosy cheeks, and bundled up in a down jacket, hood, and gloves, Melissa looked good enough to eat. Grace hugged her. "Having fun, honey?"

Melissa smiled up at her and nodded.

"The tree looks lovely, but we've got to get going, Bob."

He stood back, surveyed the tree, and smiled. Then he and Grace took the children's hands and started down Cove Road to the church.

Inside, flowers graced every table, every available nook. A fresh green velvet cover hung from the altar. Poinsettias and greenery took center stage. The Nativity manger had been freshly painted by Amelia and Mike, and sunlight streaming through the stained-glass windows filled the sanctuary with an air of holiness. Grace sat for a minute enjoying the beauty, and gave thanks for the blessings of her life.

Amelia was already there, straightening a red bow on a cluster of mums attached to the side of a pew. She moved to the vestibule, plucked a slightly bent flower from a vase on a table, and replaced it with one that stood tall and straight from a bouquet she carried on her arm. Grace soon joined her and bustled about with a flannel dust cloth in hand. She passed it over tables, pews, wherever her hawk eyes noticed a speck of dust.

Hannah sat in the vestibule going over a chart that listed the order of events. Early on, she had suggested that a seat count of the pews be taken, divided by five, and that an equal number of spaces be assigned to each of the wedding couples. This would avoid overcrowding, and folks shoving one another for seats as they tried to squeeze into pews. The couples had accepted that proposal and cooperated, limiting their invitees to the assigned number.

"There's no words to thank you ladies for what you've done here for us," Velma had said.

"It's been fun," Grace replied.

"This is the most exciting thing that's happened in Covington since we moved here," Amelia said. "I don't count the fire. That caused excitement, all right, but not of a happy kind. This is such a joyful event; I'm thrilled to be part of it."

Velma had added, "This all looks incredible. We never could have done these weddings in this short a time without you." She had hugged Grace, Hannah, and Amelia.

By one in the afternoon, Cove Road teemed with cars parked along both sides of the road, in driveways, and on lawns. Friends and relatives who had not seen one another in a long while hugged and chatted outside. They filled the pews as the pianist played soft music, and everyone waited for the brides to enter the vestibule where Hannah officiated. Excitement welled in Grace's chest as, one by one, the brides arrived and joined them there.

Then, with a rush of cold air, the vestibule door was flung open. A young man with a camera dangling from a wide strap around his neck entered. Dressed in a casual sport jacket and sneakers, he was obviously not a wedding guest.

"I'm Bill Styles from the *Appalachian News Express*." He looked from bride to bride. "Sorry we heard about your weddings so late. We have a reporter coming out, probably the day after Christmas, to talk with all of you for a big story on the Living Today page. I'm the advance guard, you might say. I'd like to get a picture of you brides to go with that story."

"How do you ladies feel about that?" Hannah asked. She moved to block his view of the brides, who nervously clustered together, whispering and glaring at the photographer.

"Ladies, how do you feel about that?" Hannah asked again.

"You all look terrific," Bill said. "It'd be great if I could get a group shot." He was speaking about the brides but looking at Hannah, since she seemed to be the one in charge.

"I don't know how I feel about having my picture plastered over the pages of a newspaper," Bernice said.

"What will people think?" Alma asked, looking at Grace.

Bernice appointed herself spokeswoman for the brides. "We don't want no newspaper reporter snooping around us or taking our pictures. We got our own photographer to take our pictures after the weddings."

He said, "I could hang around outside until your weddings are done, and when you leave the church I could be standing out there shooting candid pictures of you—maybe getting one of you with your mouth open, or turned the wrong way so you wouldn't show your best side. Or"—he paused for a moment—"I could pose you here and do a real nice shot of you, so that each one of you looks your absolute best."

"You can't take our picture without our permission, can you?" June asked.

The McCorkles, led by Bernice, advanced on Bill Styles.

They'll push him right out the door, Grace thought. She stepped between them and him. "No. Bernice, June, May—I'm sure this young man means no harm. His boss assigned him the job of coming all the way out here to take your pictures. They're interested in your story, and it's a wonderful story. Do you realize how unusual it is that five couples are being married on the same day and on Christmas Eve? This is a wonderful story for any newspaper. I'm surprised there aren't more photographers out here."

June retreated, hauling her sister with her, leaving Bernice standing before the photographer. Her hands on her hips, her face red, she said, "I don't care about none of that. I don't want my face splattered all over a newspaper."

"I think we should let him take our picture," Velma said. "Grace is right. This makes a real good story, and like he says, I'd rather show my good side and look my best."

"Okay," June said. "I agree with Velma."

"Not me." Bernice crossed her arms below her ample bosom.

Velma went to Bernice and put her arm around her shoulders. "Oh, come on, Bernice. We don't want to do this without you, and you look so lovely."

"Won't you reconsider, Bernice?" Grace asked. "Without you, the photo just won't be complete."

"Well, I'll do it just 'cause you asked me to." Pouting, Bernice followed Velma back to the others, who were beginning to adjust their skirts and jackets and check their hair and makeup in the mirror over a vestibule table.

True to his word, the photographer took his time and

posed them. He asked their names and asked each what her best side was, and he turned them to their advantage. He talked to the sisters in an easy, casual manner. "You're twins, eh?" he said to June. "Must be nice growing up with a twin."

"It was right nice. We ain't identical, as you can see, but we always got each other, and we live just two houses apart," June replied.

"And who are these adorable little girls and this young man?"

June pulled Arlene from behind her. "This is Arlene, my granddaughter. She's pretty, ain't she? She's gonna strew flower petals."

"Well, let's get her in this picture. Come on, honey," he said to the child. "You stand right here in front of your grandma."

Hesitantly, the little girl allowed him to place her in front of June.

"Perfect," he said.

Amelia handed Arlene the basket she would carry. "Just hold it, honey."

"Tip the basket a little bit forward so I can get the flower petals in the picture," Bill said. "Like this." He adjusted the basket.

Alma pushed her grandson forward. "This here is Ben. He's gonna carry our rings."

Ben hung back. His dark, curly hair fell forward into his eyes. Alma pushed it back from his face with her fingers.

"What a fine young man," the photographer said. "Let's get you in this picture."

Ida, a formidable presence in her bright blue dress, edged forward. He turned to her. "And you are?"

"The mother of two brides. The twins are mine. June was born five minutes before May."

Grace could see the pride in Ida's face.

"Well, then, mother of two brides, let's get you in the picture." He brought a chair and positioned it for Ida, and saw the other children hiding behind their grandmothers. "And who are these sweet little girls?"

"That's Lily, my youngest granddaughter," Bernice said. "She's gonna throw petals, too."

Amelia handed Lily her basket.

"And this is my Megan," Velma said. "Come stand here with me, sweetheart."

Bill's camera clicked and flashed, clicked and flashed again and again, and in a few minutes he was done, thanked them, and wished them well. Then he picked up the tripod he had not used, and whispered something to Hannah, who pointed to Amelia. Moments later, the photographer and Amelia stepped outside so that she could give him the full names of everyone.

Bernice said, "That weren't so bad. I wonder when the picture'll be in the paper?"

Grace moved from bride to bride and straightened a hat or veil here, a sleeve there, dabbed a bit of powder on Bernice's nose, cut a thread from the arm of Alma's yellow dress, and removed a tag on the back of May's suit.

"The church is gorgeous with all those flowers and everything, and you're all such beautiful brides. Everyone here will remember today and speak about it forever." She knew she would and almost wished she were one of the brides, just for the fun of it. She had shared little of her excitement about the weddings with Bob, who, always persistent, still proposing marriage after all these years, would have attempted to wheel her down the aisle in a wheelbarrow.

22

Hannah peeked into the sanctuary. Pastor Ledbetter stood before the altar, facing those gathered. She wondered if he was as calm as he appeared. He seemed confident and self-assured in his long, black robe. In his hands he held a small black book from which he would read the marriage service. Hannah gave Pastor Ledbetter a thumbs-up sign. All the grooms but one had entered the church and sat in the first row to the right. She wondered where Charlie was, then remembered that he would escort Velma.

Grace and Amelia held the doors open, and strains of the wedding march filled the church. The smell of something light and sweet, like rosewater, filled the air. Hannah beckoned to June. "It's time to start."

Amelia squeezed June's hand and handed her a bouquet of tiny red roses tied with a white ribbon. She kissed June lightly on the cheek. "You look beautiful." And to Arlene, "And you, honey. You're just so pretty. Here's your basket of petals. You just have fun, and toss them in front of you like we practiced."

Arlene took her place in front of her grandmother, exactly as rehearsed. She wore a pale green dress that swirled about her ankles. Lily of Lily's Beauty Salon had done her hair in long ringlets, and the seven-year-old looked like Shirley Temple, the child actress who had delighted so many in the nineteen forties and fifties.

Grace hugged Arlene. "Now, you just walk slow and keep those flower petals coming. Your grandma and all of us are so proud of you."

Arlene looked up at Grace and smiled, and Grace felt that old tug for the little girl she had lost in childbirth so many years ago.

"Go," Hannah whispered.

There was a swish of skirts and a shuffling of feet as men, women, and children stood and turned toward Arlene and June. The child hesitated a moment, then lifted her head and proceeded at just the right pace down the aisle. Flower petals floated for a moment in the air, then drifted to the floor.

June felt the music in every fiber of her body and moved to it. She floated, Ida walking alongside her, the bright blue dress forgotten.

Grace watched them from just inside the sanctuary, tears of happiness filling her eyes. *Three generations of women. How proud Ida must be.*

Dressed up nice in his new blue suit, Eddy stood by Pastor Denny and shuffled from leg to leg. Poor dear. June smiled at him and resisted the urge to wave to him. She also resisted the desire to giggle or skip. Alma was right. It was great to have everyone look at her, admire her, smile at her. June felt young and beautiful. Much too soon, they reached the front pew. Ida released her arm, and shepherded Arlene to the left to join Pastor Johnson in the front pew. June moved to stand alongside Eddy in the wide space between the first pew and the altar.

Pastor Denny and Pastor Johnson had discussed the service and decided that for sentimental reasons, Denny would use the service from the 1966 book of worship.

" 'Dearly beloved,' " he began. " 'We are gathered here in the sight of God, and in the presence of these witnesses to join together this man and this women in holy matrimony; which is an honorable estate, instituted of God, and signifying unto us the mystical . . .' "

The next lines June heard were " 'Wilt thou love her and keep her in sickness and health; and forsaking all others, keep thee unto her, so long as ye both shall live?' "

Eddy said, "I will."

The lines were repeated for her, and June said in a loud, clear voice, " I will."

Then came the exchange of shiny new silver rings engraved with vines that they had chosen together. Soon after, Denny was blessing them. " 'God the Father, the Son, and the Holy Spirit bless, preserve, and keep you.' "

They turned, and June saw Pastor Johnson in the front pew wiping his eyes. He looked up at her, and June smiled at him. At that moment she loved the old man, loved everyone in that church, be they friends, family, or strangers, and she was certain that they all loved her. Then hand in hand, she and Eddy moved back up the aisle.

The instant Alma stood in the doorway to the sanctuary, she lost all self-consciousness about her yellow chiffon dress. Thank the Lord she hadn't paid attention to Velma's dire predictions about the cold. She felt pretty and as happy as the dress was bright and frivolous. She did not know it, of course, but for years to come, everyone would tell her how grand she looked, and that yellow was absolutely her best color.

Alma lifted her head with pride as her youngest son guided her down the church aisle. Ahead of them, her youngest grandson bore the new rings, narrow gold bands, on a purple velvet pillow with silver tassels all around it.

Standing before the altar, Frank looked so fine and handsome up there by Pastor Ledbetter, Alma's heart skipped a beat. A second chance at something good was a wonderful thing, and when she stood alongside Frank and the service began, she counted all the blessings of her work, her home, her children and grandchildren.

She heard Pastor Denny say, "'I require and charge you both, as you stand in the presence of God, before whom the secrets of all hearts are disclosed, that, having duly considered the holy covenant you are about to make, you do now declare before this company your pledge of faith, each to the other . . .'"

She could feel the blood pounding in her temples. When the moment came, her "I will" was soft and low, but clear. Then Alma could hardly believe it was over, even when she and Frank were seated in the pew alongside June and Eddy, congratulating one another and watching Bernice start down the aisle, struggling to hold her father-in-law upright.

Bernice actually looks pretty today. Alma had never considered Bernice anything but a plain-looking girl and woman, but somehow, brides always looked pretty. Too bad she had that drunken old man hanging on her at a time like this. But Bernice seemed happy, and she'd hardly been nervous while they waited in the vestibule, except when that photographer got her all riled up. Because she had gotten to know Bernice better during these past few weeks, Alma felt more protective and interested in her. She empathized with the other woman's dislike of her weight, and wanted things to go well for her today.

Young Lily carried a basket of petals, but hardly threw any. She kept looking back, probably worried that her great-grandfather might topple and fall on her. Bernice was so distracted by her father-in-law and her anxious granddaughter that she hardly saw anyone—not her sister smiling at her, not her mother wiping her eyes and smiling, not Ralph, not the pastor, not the sunlight streaming through the stained-glass windows.

Henry McCorkle was indeed in his cups, although Ralph swore he'd been with him all the night before and that he'd been sober. He staggered along, leaning heavily on Bernice, and gasps of dismay and concern could be heard when he swayed outrageously and reached out to hold on to a pew, and instead grabbed the shoulder of the woman standing at the end.

Bernice did not feel pretty. Always self-conscious about her weight, she worried that people would think that the plain, dark dress with the wide lace collar was too stark for a wedding dress. She worried that her backside shook with every step she took, even though she had tucked herself into a brand-new and very uncomfortable panty girdle and put on panty hose, too. She felt wobbly in the high heels she was not accustomed to wearing. She felt less attractive than the other brides, and she regretted not going on down to the courthouse instead. She was afraid that everyone would gossip and laugh behind her back later.

The walk seemed endless. When Henry McCorkle stumbled into the pew near Ida and Pastor Johnson, Lily spotted her mother across the aisle and ran to her, nearly tripping Bernice. Then a relieved Bernice took her place alongside Ralph at the altar.

" 'Dearly beloved,' " Pastor Denny began.

Bernice had been to so many weddings over the years. She always cried at weddings, anyone's wedding. But she was distracted by the fact that her girdle pinched, and it seemed forever before the pastor got to the "I wills" and, finally, the blessing.

" 'God the Father, the Son, and the Holy Spirit bless, preserve, and keep you; the Lord graciously with his favor look upon you, and so fill you with all spiritual benediction and love that you may so live together in this life that in the world to come you may have life everlasting, Amen.' "

After Ralph kissed her she quickly pulled back, worried that her butt stuck out too much when she leaned forward. It was over, thank God.

May did not glow. She had let the days pass and made no arrangements with any of her children or anyone else—not an uncle or a cousin, not a friend, no one—to walk her down the aisle. Hers was not a family that spoke of personal matters much, and none of her children had inquired about her plans. Her daughters had probably assumed that she had asked one of their brothers, while the boys probably thought their mother had arranged with some other male member of the family.

Ida, sitting in the front pew, about had a fit when she realized that all of May's sons and their wives, and her daughters and their husbands, were in the pew across the aisle. May wouldn't walk down that aisle by herself, would she? That May. You never could tell what that girl would do.

Immediately Ida stood and hurried up the side aisle toward the vestibule. May was positioned at the closed door and was ready to start down the aisle. Sure enough, she was alone.

Ida demanded that she be allowed to escort her daughter.

May resisted. "Leave me alone."

Ida insisted. "It ain't proper."

"I don't care what's proper," May retorted.

"What devil's got into you, May?"

"I'm fine like I am. Leave me be, Mama."

Catching May's eye, Hannah gave the signal to begin. Grace and Amelia held the sanctuary doors open, and once again music flooded the church.

Ida grabbed May's arm. "How's it gonna look, me walking June, and you settin' off down that aisle alone? What are people gonna think about me lettin' you do that?"

And they were off. May looked up at the stained-glass windows. How beautiful they were, how soft and warm the light was, flowing through them. The walls were all so white and so clean, and the church smelled of roses.

My Lord. All these years I've spent thinking about my life, but life's not about insights and understanding. It's about getting off my duff and doing something practical, something that can actually change things. Thinking and hoping won't change a single thing for me. She searched the pews for Pastor Johnson and finally located him way up front. She'd always felt comfortable with him, and wished that he were performing this dreaded ceremony.

The tug of Ida's arm pulled her back to the task at hand, to move in sync with the music down this long aisle to the side of a man she did not love and wanted to be rid of. May's throat tightened. She considered yanking her arm from Ida's hold and running away, but she had to do this for her children's sake.

Just before the altar, Ida let go of May's arm. May did not move. Ida nudged her with her hip. "Get on up there."

The rest was a blur until Pastor Denny asked, "Who giveth this woman to be married to this man?"

Ida sprang to her feet and called, "I do."

After the vows were read, May hesitated so long before saying "I will" that Billy squeezed her hand hard. There were no new rings. The following words of the service fell like sacks of stones on her heart.

" 'I pronounce that they are husband and wife together, in the name of the Father, and of the Son, and of the Holy Spirit. Those whom God hath joined together, let no man put asunder. Amen.' Let us pray," Pastor Denny said.

Billy tugged at her until she kneeled beside him.

Denny intoned the blessing. " 'O eternal God, creator and preserver of all mankind, giver of all spiritual grace, the author of everlasting life: Send thy blessing upon this man and this woman, whom we bless in thy name, that they may surely perform and keep the vow and covenant between them made, and may ever remain in perfect love and peace together, and live according to thy laws.' "

Tears filled May's eyes. She'd no doubt hear plenty about her "attitude" from her family later, but she didn't care. She was only required to endure the ceremony, not like it.

Velma surprised them all by having Charlie escort her down the aisle. They were the oldest of the couples, happy as kids, and glowing as if they were doing this for the first time. Velma felt like a queen and Charlie her king. She had even sneaked a small tiara among the thick waves of her hair, and she nodded her head to this side and that as if she were the hostess of this grand event. If she weren't carrying a bouquet in one hand and holding Charlie's arm with the other, she would have waved to everyone.

Before them, Megan appeared to be having a great time, smiling as she strewed her flower petals.

As they had agreed, the wedding began with the usual, " 'Dearly beloved . . .' " Then, at a nod from Denny, Charlie reached into his jacket pocket and pulled out his three-by-five card. He glanced at it briefly, then fished in his jacket again but came up wanting.

"Lord, Charlie, don't tell me you forgot your glasses. How are you going to read what you've got scribbled on that card?" Velma whispered.

Denny bent forward. "Can I read it for you, or say it low so you can repeat the words?"

"No, thank you, Pastor. I know it by heart, anyway." He slipped the card back into his pocket and turned to Velma, his eyes filled with love, and his voice was clear and strong.

"Honey," he said, "I'm old. I can't see too good and not at all without those glasses I forgot. But I'm about to make promises to you that'll change my life." He grinned at her as if they were alone together, and not in an assembled congregation.

She looked at him expectantly.

"From tomorrow on, I promise not to interrupt you when you're reading. I promise to keep the TV turned low, and not shout too loud when somebody scores a touchdown. I've got to yell some, but not so loud as makes you jump out of your skin."

Light laughter came from a few of the front rows.

"I promise not to tease you no more about the freckles on your nose that you cover up with something in a jar, and I'll help you cut beans, but I won't stay to can them."

By now people were whispering.

Charlie raised his voice. "And I promise that when I come to this here church for Sunday service or holidays, I'll be respectful and not chat with my neighbor, even in a whisper." He clasped both of Velma's hands, leaned forward, and kissed her softly on the lips.

A soft murmur swept through the church.

Then Charlie said, "I've enjoyed the best years of my life with you, honey. I love you, and plan to just keep on loving you."

Women dabbed their eyes and sniffled.

Denny said, "Will you, Charlie Paul Herrill, take Velma Anne Benson Herrill to be your lawful wedded wife?"

"I sure will, Pastor." Charlie pulled out the velvet box and placed a ring on Velma's finger.

Velma cleared her throat. How could she even speak after listening to her husband's loving words? She wanted to hug him and hold him close to her, right here and now.

"Charlie, you've been a good husband to me and a good father to our children," she began. "You've been there for us in good times and bad. Just like I've been doing all these years, I promise to go on loving and cherishing you for the rest of our lives—whether you help me with the canning or not." She paused. There was more she wanted to say, but if she did she would cry. She'd say it all to Charlie when they were alone tonight instead.

"Do you, Velma Anne Benson Herrill, take Charlie Paul Herrill to be your lawful wedded husband?" Denny asked.

"I most certainly will."

She slipped the other ring onto Charlie's finger, then kissed her husband's cheek. They faced one another holding hands, smiling at each another.

Denny raised his hands above their heads. "Then, in the power vested in me by God and by the state of North Carolina, I declare you man and wife."

"Amen," someone called.

Someone else clapped loudly, and then everyone joined in.

Velma and Charlie turned and moved back up the aisle, oblivious to anyone but each other.

23

Charlie and Velma joined the other newlyweds in the vestibule, and the church came alive with chatter as the guests crowded the aisle, and family members surrounded the newlywed couples to hug and kiss and wish them well.

Without the help of Grace, Hannah, and Amelia, Mike would never have managed to herd the newlyweds back into the now-empty church, where he had set up his camera equipment for their wedding pictures. There was not much time, with the Christmas Eve service soon to follow.

Their sons and daughters and grandchildren joined them inside, positioned by Amelia with Grace's help and instructed to smile. The photo sessions took less than an hour, and as each family finished, they departed to join their relatives and friends at the receptions that would follow.

Bernice had invited the ladies to the McCorkles' reception, which would be held at Bernice and Ralph's large farmhouse set back in the foothills of McCorkle Creek.

"It's a covered-dish supper. We got plenty of food, so you ladies don't bring nothing," she reminded them as she left the church. "May, June, and all their families are gonna be there, and we got some mighty fine cooks. Pastor Denny and Pastor Johnson are coming after they finish doing the Christmas Eve service. I know you all gotta go to Velma and Alma's party, too, but come to ours first and bring Miss Lurina."

Hannah, Grace, Max, Bob, and Lurina arrived at Bernice and Ralph's home just as the music started. A country rock band in the large living room filled the house with music that blasted out into the yard. Trucks and cars of all shapes and sizes lined both sides of the road, leaving a narrow lane for Bob's SUV to squeeze through.

A boy who looked maybe fourteen appeared, introduced himself as Cliff McCorkle, Bernice's nephew, and offered to park their car. "We got spaces left up behind the barn," he said.

Bob hesitated. "You'll find me and give me back my keys?"

"I sure will," Cliff replied, and took the keys. Moments later he revved the engine and took off, turned right sharply, and headed toward the huge barn.

Inside, competing with the music and definitely winning, a long buffet table groaned under the weight of food: huge platters of fried chicken, ham and red-eye gravy, collard greens, green beans cooked with ham, sweet potatoes, mashed white potatoes, corn, biscuits and gravy, corn bread, and more. The table was pulled out from the wall to allow for two lines, and twenty people on each side were lined up with plates in their hands.

After a time, the two pastors arrived. Bernice had changed into a bright red flowing dress that came to her ankles, and was in her glory as hostess. She told May, "Now you take these here plates to the ministers, and see that Pastor Johnson don't have to get up for nothing."

The ministers sat side by side on a sofa, Denny a bit stiffly, Grace thought. Pastor Johnson looked better than he had in weeks and seemed stimulated by the activity around him. He appeared to enjoy the attention he received from everyone, even the children, who hung on the back of the sofa and whispered into his ear. After they ate and chatted some more, Pastor Johnson and Denny finally gave way to exhaustion, excused themselves and departed.

At the covered-dish supper at Velma's home, Grace, Hannah, Amelia, their menfolk, and Lurina joined the Craines and Herrills and their families and friends at a more subdued reception, where soft Christmas music played in the background. Again the buffet table groaned beneath the weight of food, and Alma had hired a storyteller from Asheville, a tall lady with graying hair that hung to her waist and a long robelike dress, who spun yarn after yarn, some funny, some sad.

Lurina listened, enchanted. "You mean that there woman gets paid for tellin' stories?" she asked Grace when they got home. She would spend the night in the ladies' guest room.

"Yes. She's a professional storyteller."

"I coulda been one of them, couldn't I, Grace?"

"You are one of them," Grace replied as she helped Lurina off with her dress. "Your stories are as interesting as any she told tonight."

The dress came off, and Lurina sighed with relief. "If I was younger and starting out telling stories at schools and parties today, I'd get paid, too, wouldn't I?" Lurina asked, her tone wistful.

"Indeed you could," Grace assured Lurina, holding her flannel nightgown while Lurina slipped her arms into it.

Lurina patted Grace's arm. "You're a good girl, Grace. I had a specially fine time today. Thanks for asking me along."

"It was a very special day, and you were a great help to us. Everyone appreciated having you there. I love you, Lurina." Grace hugged her.

The tiny old woman clung to Grace, holding her close. "The Lord sure blessed me when He sent you into my life," Lurina said.

24

❧

Much later, after the party was over, after everyone's well-wishes and hugs and kisses, Velma and Charlie lay in bed. Velma snuggled close to him under the quilt in the big bed that had been her grandmother's.

"It's like a miracle. Who would have imagined that the church would get painted and be so beautiful, and that we'd have a new heater installed in such a short time, and that five of us couples would get remarried together? Bless Grace and Hannah and Amelia for all the help they gave us. We couldn't have done it without them."

"And the men, Max, Bob, and Mike, were a huge help. Denny's working out well, too. Folks like him. He did a nice job with the weddings. He gave each couple just what they wanted."

"And Pastor Johnson's looking a whole heap better, don't you think?"

"Having someone who cares about him to look after

him makes a world of difference." Charlie drew her closer.

"I sure know about that. Having you here to love and care about me is the best thing in my life," she said.

"You are all I ever want or need, Velma. God blessed us with each other, don't you think?"

She nodded and kissed him. "And with our kids, too."

"And we're all legal now, and so are they, and we don't have to worry about that anymore."

Velma smiled. "Makes me feel all warm and happy inside."

They lay there in the darkness, filled with a sense of well-being, grateful for their lives and for each other. "So all's well that ends well," Charlie said, and kissed her good night.

Holiday Recipes

⚜

Blueberry Banana Smoothie

1 cup of milk (1%, skim, or 2%)
1 cup fat-free plain yogurt
1 cup of blueberries
$\frac{1}{2}$ banana that has been frozen
2 tablespoons of Splenda

Place milk in blender. Add yogurt, blueberries, banana, and Splenda. Substitute strawberries or raspberries for blueberries, if desired. Blend until creamy. If too thick, add a small amount of milk. If used as a dessert, pour blended mixture into Pyrex cups and place in fridge for an hour before serving to thicken. Decorate with a sprig of fresh mint on top.

Makes 2 eight-ounce glasses, if used as a drink, or 4 dessert servings.

Carmen's Holiday Curried Fruit (highly recommended)

> 1 large can each of halved peaches and pears
> 1 large can of pineapple slices
> $1/4$ cup melted butter
> $1/4$ cup light brown sugar
> 3 teaspoons curry powder—less if you prefer a lighter curry
>   taste
> 1 small bottle maraschino cherries

Drain fruit well and pat dry with paper towels. Melt butter. Remove from heat, and mix in curry and brown sugar. Place fruit facedown in a 7 x 11 (approximately) casserole. Sprinkle sugar mixture over fruit. Bake uncovered at 325 degrees for one hour. Can be served hot or cold—Carmen likes it hot.

Carmen suggests that after baking, you place a pineapple ring on each peach and pear and top with a cherry. Wonderful side dish with ham.

Makes 10 servings.

Cold Cherry Soup

2 sixteen-oz. cans of pitted sour cherries (do not drain)
3 tablespoons of Splenda or sugar
1 slice of seeded lemon
2 teaspoons of cornstarch or arrowroot
4 tablespoons of sour cream

Place cherries and liquid from can in a saucepan. Add sugar or Splenda and lemon and simmer for 4–5 minutes. Remove from heat. In a small bowl, mix cornstarch or arrowroot and sour cream very well. Add to cherries. Stir over low heat (do not boil), using a wooden spoon until thickened. Cool and chill soup. Add lemon for a tarter taste, or Splenda or sugar to sweeten.

Serve cold in glass bowls.

Makes 6 servings.

Discussion Questions

1. Discuss the reactions of each of the women to the fact that they were not legally married.

2. How do you think you would react if you were to discover you were not married to your husband of many years?

3. Were you pleased with the outcome of the story?

4. Were you pleased with the role each lady played?

5. What would you have done differently?

6. In your opinion, did May McCorkle do the right thing? Did she, do you think, have a choice?

7. Were you comfortable with Pastor Denny as a surrogate for Pastor Johnson? If so, why? If not, why?